That time, he r͏ obvious disd͏a "You're not going to res͏o͏r͏t͏ ͏t͏o͏ ͏͏ ͏͏e you, doc?" he said, giving me another of those more penetrating stares. "...Not so soon in our new friendship? I haven't intimidated you already, have I?" At my silence, his voice grew bored. "The constant repetition of my given name. The clinical yet polite peppering of questions in an attempt to quietly undermine my sense of autonomy here..."

"Fine." I held up both of my palms in a gesture of surrender. "What do you want to talk about, Mr. Black? Do you want to tell me what you were doing at the Palace of Fine Arts earlier this morning?"

"Not here," he said cryptically, smiling at me again.

I frowned, glancing around the gunmetal gray room.

"Somewhere else, then?" I said.

"Yes," he said. "For all of your questions, doc. Including the ones I wouldn't answer before."

I gave him another puzzled smile. "I hate to tell you, Mr. Black, but you're not likely to be anyplace that is significantly different from this room anytime soon. Not in terms of a non-institutional setting...if that's what you're driving at."

"It must certainly appear that way to you, yes," he said, raising his chained wrists for emphasis and glancing around the room with those gold eyes. "...But perhaps you are mistaken in that, doc. Perhaps you'll find that we can speak in a much more comfortable setting, just the two of us...and in not too long a time."

I narrowed my gaze at him.

It didn't sound like a threat, at least not coming from him. But the words themselves could definitely have been construed as one.

I gave him a wry smile. "You think so, huh?"

I do, a voice said clearly in my mind. *I do think so, doc...*

BLACK IN WHITE

A Quyentin Black Paranormal Mystery

by

JC ANDRIJESKI

White Sun Press

BLACK IN WHITE
A Quentin Black Paranormal Mystery

Copyright 2016 by JC Andrijeski
(Ebook copyright in 2015)
Published by White Sun Press

First Edition

ISBN-13: 978-1545436714
ISBN-10: 1545436711

Cover Art & Design by Damonza
http://damonza.com
2016

Link with me at: jcandrijeski.com

Or at: www.facebook.com/JCAndrijeski/

Mailing List: http://hyperurl.co/JCA-Newsletter

White Sun Press
For more information
about any book published by White Sun Press, please go to
www.whitesunpress.com

Printed in the United States of America
2016

DEDICATED TO MY FATHER
(in the hopes he never reads it)
...who is also a riddle wrapped in a mystery inside an enigma
wrapped in a fortune cookie.

Sorry I never bought you that plane.

PROLOGUE
PALACE

FIFTEEN-YEAR-OLD JANINE RICO WAS HAVING A GOOD NIGHT.

Scratch that.

She was having a *great* night.

An epically awesome night, by pretty much any standard.

First of all, getting alcohol was easy, for a change. She and her pals Hannah and Keeley managed to shoulder-tap some epically challenged, can-I-come-party-with-you-kids loser on their very first try, outside a seedy liquor store on Fillmore. The owner, an older Indian man, didn't care—so loser boy emerged five minutes later with one of the big bottles of peppermint schnapps and another of cheap rum. They ditched him in the park minutes later, running off with two guys from their school and laughing their asses off.

That was like, hours ago now.

The boys had gone home.

They'd been wandering the city most of the night since, determined to make the most of Keeley's mom being out of town and letting them stay in her condo in the Marina District. They'd stopped at a few parks to pass the bottles around and talk and snap pictures with their smart phones, watching the orange-tinted fog billow in odd, smoke-like exhales across the wet grass. They'd already discussed their plans for the next day... which mostly involved sleeping in, along with ordering pizza and movies with Keeley's mom's credit card.

An epic weekend, all in all. Awesomely flawless.

Janine was tired now, though. The cold wind cut her too, even through the down jacket she wore over her hoodie sweatshirt and multicolored knit tights.

It was Keeley's idea to stop at the Palace of Fine Arts before they headed back.

"Nooooo," Janine whined, flopping her arms dramatically. "I'm ready to pass out. I'm cold. I have to pee...this is stupid!"

"Come on," Keeley cajoled. "It's totally cool! Look...it's all lit up!"

"It's lit up every night," Janine grumbled.

Hannah hooked Janine's arm, but sided with Keeley. "We can take pictures...send them to Kristi in Tahoe and make her *crazy* jealous!"

Hannah always wanted to dig at Kristi. Maybe because Kristi's family was rich, or maybe because Hannah was jealous that Kristi and Janine were best friends.

Either way, Janine couldn't fight both of them.

Her eyes shifted to the orange-lit, fifty-foot-tall, Roman-esque columns. They stood on the other side of a man-made lake covered in sleeping ducks and swans, making a disjoined crescent like ancient ruins from an old amphitheater. The fountain in the lake was turned off, so the columns reflected a near-perfect mirror on the glass surface of the water.

As they tromped over slippery grass, Janine found herself thinking it did look pretty cool, with the robe-draped stone ladies resting their arms on top of each column, showing their stone backs to the world. Broken by deep black shadows, the stone faces looked otherworldly. Willow trees hung over the lake, rustling over the water as the wind lifted their pale leaves.

"All right," she mumbled, rolling her eyes to let them know they owed her.

Hannah broke out the last of the peppermint schnapps, handing around the bottle by the neck. Shivering and pulling her down jacket tighter against the wind, Janine took a long drink, choking a bit. The warmth of the burn was welcome.

She thought about school on Monday, and telling the other kids about their night.

Hannah was right. This was *so* going to blow Kristi's mind.

Cheered at the thought, Janine grinned, taking another slug of the schnapps and shuddering when it wanted to come back up her throat.

"I think I'm done," she said, handing the bottle to Keeley and wiping her mouth.

"I soooo want to get married here!" Keeley said, after taking her own drink.

"Me too!" Hannah seconded.

The three of them wandered the asphalt path between orange-lit columns. The path led to the rotunda, but would also spit them out through the row of columns on the other side, and back to the lawn that would eventually let them off at the edge of the Marina District.

Maybe this wasn't such a bad short cut after all.

The columns looked way bigger and taller up close, like something really and truly old. Janine gawked up with her two friends, despite the dozens of times she'd walked here with her parents or during school trips or whatever.

Pulling out her smart phone, she took a few pictures, first

3

just of the columns themselves, then of Keeley and Hannah as they posed, hanging on the base of pillars and stone urn.

"We should send these to Kristi *now!*" Hannah squealed, laughing with her arm slung around Keeley's neck. "She will be *sooo* pissed!"

"No, her mom checks her phone, like, every day," Janine warned. "She would totally bust us if she saw what time we'd sent these."

Hannah's expression sobered. Before she could answer, they all came to an abrupt stop.

Keeley saw it first.

She smacked Janine, who came to a dead stop, right before Janine grabbed Hannah, gripping her friend's peacoat jacket in a tightly-clenched fist.

Hannah froze.

Before them, a woman wearing a white, flowing dress lay in a strangely elegant pose on the ground. Something about the way her legs and arms were positioned struck Janine as broken-looking, despite the precision...like a store mannequin that had been accidentally knocked over and lay facing the wrong direction.

The woman's legs were almost in a running or leaping pose. Her arms curved up over her head, the wrists and fingers positioned inward like a ballerina's. Her chin and face tilted up, towards the lake, as if to look between her delicately positioned hands.

Whatever caused the position, it didn't look right.

The woman's face didn't look right, either.

It belonged to a porcelain doll. Someone had slathered so much make-up on her cheeks and eyes that they appeared bruised.

4

Those details, however, Janine remembered only later.

In those few seconds, all she could see was the blood.

The woman's dress from waist to bust-line was soaked a dark red that looked purple in the orange light under the dome. That same splash of red covered her all the way to her thighs, past where the dress bunched up and flared out like the dress of a princess in fairytale.

It was a wedding dress.

The teenagers just stood there, all three of them breathing hard now, like they'd been running. They stared at the woman under the Palace of Fine Arts rotunda as if the sight put them in a trance.

Janine found herself unable to look away.

Then she realized they weren't alone.

Next to the woman in white, a man crouched, staring down at her.

Janine must have seen him there.

She must have been staring right at him, along with the woman. Even so, his form seemed to jump out at her all at once.

Her first, irrational thought was: *He must be the groom.*

Then Janine saw his hands reach for the mid-section of the woman on the ground.

He was touching her.

His face remained in shadow. Black hair hung down over his eyes. He straightened in a single, fluid motion and like the woman in white, blood streaked his skin like glistening paint, all the way past his elbows to the edges of his black T-shirt.

His face and neck wore dark and shining splotches of the same.

He turned his head, staring at the three girls.

For the first time, the angles of his face caught the light, displaying high cheekbones and a distinct lack of expression in the sunset-colored flood lamps aimed at the dome. Those almond-shaped eyes looked oddly yellow — almost gold — under that glow of the rotunda.

Janine saw those feral-looking eyes focus on Hannah, then Keeley.

Right before they aimed directly at her.

Her trance finally broke.

A loud, familiar-sounding voice let out a piercing scream. The scream echoed inside the hollow chamber of the dome, replicating there.

It occurred to Janine only later that the scream came from her.

That was *her* screaming, Janine Rico.

In the same instant, a voice rose in her mind.

This one didn't sound like her at all.

Run away, little girl, the voice whispered. *Run away now, little one, all the way home, before the big bad wolf decides to eat you, too...*

Janine didn't have to be told twice.

ONE
SUSPECT

YOU'VE GOT TO GET A LOAD OF THIS GUY, MIRIAM," NICK told me that morning, leaning against the jamb of my office door and grinning. "You really do. He's a *serious* piece of work...like..." He made a motion by the side of his head with his fingers, expanding them out sharply, like his own brain just exploded. "...Total head job. Right up your alley."

I scowled.

It was seven in the morning.

I hadn't even managed to finish my first cup of coffee yet.

Inspector Naoko "Nick" Tanaka hadn't bothered with a hello first, when he showed up at the door of my inner office. He was also there an hour before reception opened, not like that ever stopped him. I knew Gomey was out there too, as in Gomez Ramirez, my so-called administrative assistant and personal pain in my ass. And yeah, I knew Nick was a pushy bastard who never knocked, never asked permission, but it still bugged me that Gomey hadn't even *tried* to stop him. He could have warned me at least.

I combed my fingers through my long black hair and sighed, looking up at Nick with what I hoped was a flat-eyed stare. I hadn't even put on make-up yet, telling myself I'd do it in the office bathroom before my first client. I could pull off the no make-up thing better than most, I knew — thanks to inheriting my mom's Native American skin tone and good bone structure and dark eyelashes — but I still felt a little naked without it. I'd left my hair down too, and for some reason, that always made me feel a bit too visibly female at work.

Truthfully, I felt unprepared to deal with anyone this early, even Nick, who I'd known forever. I hadn't donned my professional armor yet.

Nick took his weight off the doorjamb, all five-foot-eleven of him, most of it solid muscle.

He looked tired, I couldn't help noticing.

I assessed his overall mental state out of rote, more occupational hazard than because I meant to do it. Tired, and more stressed out than usual, even if he was doing his usual and hiding it under a grin and his own professional armor, that of the swaggering, b.s.-talking cop. I knew that armor was partly calculated. I also knew it worked, in that people who didn't know him constantly underestimated him. Nick knew I saw through it of course, but he couldn't help himself.

He lingered in my doorway for a few seconds more before entering all the way.

I don't know if he'd been waiting for an invitation or just letting me get used to the fact he was there. Nick, being a homicide cop, wasn't dumb about psychology either.

Technically, that was my bailiwick, though.

I'm not a forensic psychologist by training, but somehow I ended up one — a *de facto* one at least — and most of that was Nick's fault, too.

Technically I'm a clinical and research psychologist, and

honestly, I tried my damnedest to stick to the research side of that as much as humanly possible.

Nick and I had history, though.

He'd even introduced me to my current boyfriend (now fiancé, I reminded myself)...Ian. Ian was another old military buddy of Nick's. They met in Iraq, though — not Afghanistan like me and Nick. I'd gone in later than Nick, being over a decade younger.

Since Ian was British and worked in intelligence, not the regular armed forces, he and I never crossed paths over there. We met after Ian moved to San Francisco over a year ago and Nick took us all out for drinks, thinking me and Ian might hit it off.

Well, that was Nick's story, anyway.

Ian told me that the drinks had been his idea. He claimed he'd pushed Nick for an introduction after seeing a picture of me on Nick's mantle in his crappy apartment in South San Francisco.

Either way, Nick and I had history.

And Nick might be a cop now, but he still thought like a guy in a firefight.

I watched Nick do his cop-walk into my personal space, wearing a rumpled black suit with a dark blue shirt underneath. Only then did I notice the splattering of stains on the front of his suit, visible under the heavier motorcycle jacket he wore over it.

I frowned, trying to identify the exact stains.

They didn't look like coffee. Even so, the more conscious part of my mind refused to acknowledge the "blood" categorization that popped into my head.

So yeah, Nick was tired, wound up, and he had blood on him.

He put his hands on his hips, which rumpled both jackets

enough that I saw the handle of his Glock poke out from where he had it in a shoulder holster on his right side. I noticed he'd cut his midnight-black hair shorter than usual on the back and sides, but left it longer in front.

Even exhausted, he still looked good, did Nick Tanaka. Even at this ungodly hour.

Unfortunately, he knew it.

So did the women he burned through on a monthly or sometimes weekly basis.

Not me, though.

I'd become part of Nick's inner circle, one of his go-to people when he was working a case, like an oddly-shaped tool in his tool box that he pulled out when he found the right-sized bolt that needed unscrewing.

I'd already known something was going on at the station.

Whatever it was, it had a lot of people excited. I'd heard smatterings on my way into the office, mostly via low-voiced conversations while I stood in line for my daily dose of high-octane coffee from The Royale Blend, the gourmet coffee shop that lived in the storefront directly below my office. Since my office is located just a few blocks from the Northern District police station, I share the same coffee shop with a lot of the cops that work out of there.

Well, the cops willing to fork over four bucks for a decent cup of coffee.

Still, even though I knew something was up, I was surprised to see Nick here already.

Usually he didn't need me this early.

"Seriously," Nick said, grinning at me as he assessed me with his dark brown eyes. "I can't wait to get your diagnosis, doc." He gave his head a theatrical shake. The smile didn't entirely mask the tenser look I glimpsed underneath. "This guy...wow. You're going to get a kick out of him, Miri. Assuming you can get him to talk to you at all."

I arched an eyebrow, giving him my best clinical stare.

"You think he's mentally unfit?" I said. "On what diagnosis?"

As per usual, he totally blew past my sarcasm.

"On the diagnosis that I think he's a total nutcase," Nick said, grinning at me. He pulled a toothpick out the back row of his white teeth, a habit I'd told him more than once was disgusting. I grimaced now as he tossed the frayed piece of wood into my trash can. "...That's my expert opinion, doc. No charge. But I still want you to talk to him. If I could nail this guy without him dropping down into an insanity plea, I'd sleep better at night."

Given that I was still nursing my first cup of coffee, I wasn't sharp enough yet to get anything but annoyed at the glint of denser meaning in his dark eyes.

Then again, I've always hated cagey, hinting crap.

It even annoyed me coming from Nick.

Despite the tiredness I could see around his eyes and the blood on his shirt and suit jacket, Nick looked amped up and almost on edge, even for him. I knew Nick ran every day before work. He left his apartment like clockwork at four a.m.—unless he happened to be working, like today. He also surfed, at least on the mornings he didn't get called in, and was a member of the same martial arts club as me.

Unlike me, Nick also lifted weights, went mountain biking, played basketball.

He was one of *those* cops.

He also lived almost entirely for his job. Nick was in his early forties at least, but he'd never been married, which probably helped with the near-singular focus.

He was just one of those intense, burn-the-candle-at-both-ends kind of guys.

Driven, I guess would be the non-clinical word.

I continued to cradle my coffee cup for a few seconds more, not moving in the half-broken down, leather office chair I still hadn't managed to get Gomey to either fix or declare dead and replace. Glancing around at the papers strewn across my desk and the filled-to-overflowing in-box with its beat up manilla and dark green folders,

I could only sigh.

My one and only office plant looked like it was screaming silently at me, possibly in its death throes since it had been so long since I'd remembered to water it.

I knew Gomey hadn't been doing that, either.

"Why?" I said finally, when all Nick did was grin at me. "What's his deal?"

"Oh, don't let me spoil it..."

"Seriously?" I said. "What are we, twelve?"

"Trust me," Nick said. "You'll want to talk to this one in person, Miri. I don't want to say anything until you see him. I don't want to...bias anything."

Realizing he wasn't going to let me off the hook, and further, that he was actually *waiting* for me, expecting me to just drop everything I hadn't yet started for the day and follow him to whatever piss-smelling interrogation room where they were holding this clown, I sighed again.

"You can't give me a few minutes?" I said.

"No."

"I have an appointment coming in at nine, Nick."

Frowning, Nick looked at his watch, as if a ticking bomb were counting down somewhere in another part of the building.

"Any chance you could cancel it?" he said apologetically, shifting his feet. "We're pretty sure he's the guy on the thing last week. That mess at Grace Cathedral."

I glanced up sharper at that.

He meant the wedding guy.

Once more glimpsing the more serious look behind the humor in Nick's eyes, I nodded my defeat and rose to standing from behind the broken chair.

Sadly, I guess there's a reason Nick counts on me.

I'm a sucker.

THERE WASN'T A LOT OF PRE-WORK ON THIS ONE.

Well, not yet.

No one wanted to debrief me on much in the way of details, presumably because Nick told them not to. So I didn't get handed the usual cobbled-together file of scribbled notes and photos and whatever else from the preliminary interrogations, or much in the way of details of what they'd found at the actual scene.

Nick gave me the bare bones story only.

Three fifteen-year-old girls stumbled upon the suspect at the scene of the crime. According to them, he'd been covered in blood. He also looked like he'd just finished — or maybe remained deep in the process of — doing "something" to a woman's dead body. Their testimony was pretty vague on details, according to Nick.

He admitted to me that he couldn't really get a sense if they'd seen *anything* concrete, apart from the suspect himself...as well

as the victim, a white dress, a lot of make-up and a lot of blood...
all of which were damning enough, under the circumstances.

Well, that and what had been done to the victim herself.

I only got the bare bones on that, too, and didn't ask for
more. Truthfully, I've never gotten used to seeing that kind of
thing, not even in pictures.

The three girls ran like hell once the suspect spotted them.

Even so, more than an hour passed before they called in what
they'd seen, although they freely admitted they all had smart
phones with them at the time. The latter had been confirmed by
the presence of photos they'd taken on the walkway leading up
to the Palace before they reached the dome where the body had
been displayed.

From what Nick told me, the delay on calling had more to
do with the girls' fears of getting caught by their parents than
fear of the suspect himself, who hadn't bothered to chase them.
Something about being out all night and drunk while crashing
at the home of an out-of-town parent. Nick said they admitted to
arguing amongst themselves about what to do after they arrived
back at a Marina residence.

They finally called it in around five o'clock.

A black and white had already picked up the suspect by
then, as it turned out.

They saw him crossing Marina Boulevard towards the
promenade, presumably to reach the coast. Bad luck on his part,
Nick said with a wry grin. He figured the guy had been heading
for the yacht harbor north of the Palace of Fine Arts, either to hop
a boat or to wash off the blood, or maybe both. If he'd succeeded
in either, they might never have got him.

As it was, they pulled guns on him to get him to comply.

From what I could tell, they pretty much lifted this guy off the street and parked him in an interrogation room while they called the coroner and forensics to the scene of the murder. I knew someone must have talked to him...and likely cleaned him up...probably Nick and whatever officer arrived first on the scene.

But they couldn't have gone through the whole range of the usual song and dance, either.

Which meant Nick was bending the rules a little, bringing me in now.

I knew Nick had a tendency to pull me in when he had a gut feeling, so I figured that must be the case with this guy, too.

Despite the overwhelming evidence, at least in terms of the Palace of Fine Arts murder, Nick probably wanted me to help him crawl into the guy's head, maybe so he could get a sense of his connection to the Grace Cathedral killings, or maybe to build evidence against an insanity plea, like he said.

Maybe he liked him for other, possibly-related crimes.

They'd do the DNA testing thing and everything else, of course, but Nick tended to be thorough. He probably wanted me to confirm or deny his working profile on the guy before he started running up blind alleys.

I peered through the one-way glass of the interrogation room, sipping my now lukewarm coffee and trying to assess the scene before me objectively.

"So you like this guy for the Grace Cathedral murders?" I said, as much to myself as Nick, who stood right at my arm.

"I like this guy for Jimmy Hoffa," Nick said, glancing at his partner, Glen Frakes, who snorted from the other side of him. "I like him for the Zodiac killings...and the death of my Aunt Lanai in Tokyo, God rest her soul."

Rolling my eyes, I nodded, getting the gist.

I continued to look through the one-way glass, trying to get a sense of what I might be in for when I went in there.

The guy just sat there, not moving.

I don't think I'd ever seen anyone sit so still in an interrogation room before.

His eyes didn't dart to either the door or the cameras, which just about everyone looked at, seemingly without being able to help themselves.

No one liked being watched.

No one liked being trapped inside a featureless room, either.

This guy wasn't trying to be clever, either, staring at us through the one-way glass, which a lot of them did to show us they *knew* they were being watched.

Nick's suspect didn't seem to care.

I got nothing. A blank wall.

That didn't happen to me very often, truthfully.

Maybe thirty, thirty-five years old.

Muscular. Obviously in good shape, but not bulky like Nick with his weight-lifting and kung fu and judo and whatever else. This guy had the lean musculature of a runner or a fighter, not an ounce of excess flesh on him anywhere. I'd seen criminals and even addicts with that kind of body type of course, but I wasn't getting any of the other signs of career criminal or addiction or living on the street on Nick's new favorite perp.

His eyes were clear, as was his skin, which was on the tanned side, but still light enough to be ethnically ambiguous. He looked healthy. He was handsome, actually, if in a feral kind of way. He had black hair, high cheekbones, a well-formed mouth, and some of the lightest, strangest-colored eyes I'd ever seen...so light they looked gold, and strangely flecked.

Those eyes reminded me of a tiger. Or maybe a mountain

lion...or an *actual* lion...although I couldn't remember what color eyes either of those had in real life.

Even those oddly riveting eyes weren't the most noticeable thing about Nick's new friend. Not at that precise moment, anyway.

No, the most noticeable thing about him *now* was that he was covered in blood. Unlike with Nick, I couldn't even pretend to not know what it was.

A good portion of his visible bare skin wore a mostly-dry layer of reddish-brown smears and spots. It covered his hands and arms from his fingertips up to his rock-hard biceps, just below the cuffs of the stretchy black T-shirt he wore, which also accentuated the size of his chest. More smears and splatters of the same covered his neck and one side of his face. I could see it on the rings he wore, where his wrists were cuffed together and resting on the metal table.

I also saw blood smearing the face of his military-style watch.

I wasn't an expert of course, but even if Nick hadn't already told me how they'd found him on the street, I would have known just by looking at him. It was definitely blood.

He'd practically been bathing in it, this guy.

It explained how Nick came to have it on his own shirt, too.

The suspect's clothes, which included that form-fitting black T-shirt, black pants and black leather shoes, the last of which I could just see under the table, absorbed most of the color and texture of what decorated his bare skin. I'd already been assured by Nick and Glen that blood covered a good portion of his clothes, too, visible or not.

I was kind of surprised they hadn't stripped him yet, to pull evidence.

They'd even left his shoes, rings and watch, which was unusual when they had a suspect cuffed like this and chained to the floor.

As if he'd read my mind, Nick said, "We've got forensics coming up here in an hour. They're at the scene now. We thought we'd give you a look first...while we wait."

I gave Nick a skeptical stare.

That time, he had the grace to blush.

"Okay," he said, holding up his hands in a gesture of surrender. "*I* wanted you to look at him, Miriam. He won't talk to us. I thought you might be able to give me some suggestions. Before we go all Guantanamo on his ass."

Frowning, I pursed my lips.

Then I looked back at Nick's blood-covered suspect.

That time, I tried to push aside the emotional impact of the blood and assess the man himself. I still couldn't get anything off him in the usual way. Even so, his war-paint aside, he had something about him, this guy. I couldn't put my finger on what it was, not in those first few seconds, but I found it difficult to look away from his face. He looked surprisingly calm, and those odd-colored eyes shone with intelligence.

If anything, he looked alert.

Not quite waiting, but expectant...even as he seemed to be using the time in some more complex mental exercise I couldn't see. That sharpness he wore had a calculating quality, as if he were otherwise occupied in some further reach of his mind.

I also distinctly got military.

Only after I'd been looking at him for a few seconds more did I realize that the alertness told me more about his demeanor than the calm he wore over it. Something about that calm of his was deceptive, in fact. Behind it, he looked high-strung.

18

Like, *really* high-strung.

Like he was remaining where he sat through sheer force of will.

I reassessed my "not a drug addict" summation briefly, but then went back to my original conclusion a few seconds later. What I was seeing didn't come from drugs. He looked like he wanted to be elsewhere, without looking the slightest bit afraid, or nervous, or even angry. He didn't look smug, either, like most psychopaths I'd seen.

Instead, he seemed to view his being here as a colossal waste of his time.

Once I'd seen that, I couldn't un-see it. Further, it occurred to me that he didn't even seem to be hiding his impatience particularly well.

I might have noticed it before if I hadn't been trying so hard to read him in other ways.

"What's his name?" I said.

Again, Nick and Glen exchanged a look.

"What?" I said. "What's the joke now?"

"If you can get a name out of that guy, I'll buy you dinner," Nick said. Grinning, he gave me a teasing once-over. "Of course, I'd do that for free, doc...just name the day."

Glen snorted again, folding his thick arms over his chest.

Raising my left hand to Nick in what had recently become a running joke with us, I tapped my engagement ring with my thumb. Nick grinned, feigning disappointment, then motioned with his head towards the man sitting in the other room. My eyes followed his stare back to the guy with the flecked, gold-colored eyes, even as Nick's voice grew more openly cop-like.

"He won't give us a name. No ID on him. His prints aren't in the system."

"Mystery guy, huh?" I said.

I said it casually, even with a lilt of humor. Still, I was puzzled. Television aside, that almost never happened, not anymore.

You couldn't get anywhere anymore without some kind of ID.

"We're running facial rec on him now," Nick said, almost like he heard me. "We'll give him to Interpol if we don't find him here. He's got to have at least an alias...somewhere."

"No military record?" I said.

"Nothing on the books."

I nodded, only half-hearing him as I frowned at the suspect. Nothing. He really was a blank wall.

That was pretty rare for me, like I said.

Not unheard of, but yeah...rare.

"What makes you think he'll talk to *me?*" I said finally, looking back at Nick.

Nick just smiled, shifting his weight on his feet.

"He probably won't," Glen volunteered from Nick's other side. "But Nicky here seems to think you walk on water, doc, so he wanted to give it a shot."

Shrugging, even as I gave Nick an annoyed look, I tossed my paper cup of coffee in the plastic-lined bin under the desk and made a somewhat overdone motion towards the other room.

"Well?" I said. "We might as well kill time until forensics shows up, right? I canceled my morning's slate for this dog and pony show."

I added that last part with more bite, giving Nick a harder stare.

Grinning at me, Glen, who was a good five inches taller than Nick and built like a linebacker, or maybe some kind of throwback to his Viking roots, nodded. Motioning for me to follow, he aimed his feet for the door so he could let me inside the interrogation room.

As I walked past him, though, Nick caught hold of my upper arm.

"Don't fool around with this guy," he warned.

The smile vanished from Nick's face, leaving my friend, the guy I knew behind his schtick.

I remembered that look from Afghanistan, too.

"...I mean it, Miri. He's probably a serial killer. At the very least, he likes dead bodies a little too much. We'll be right outside that door. If you want out, get out. Right away. Don't play tough for the cop crowd...hear me?"

Normally I would have chewed him out for the whole damsel-needing-protection crap, which I thought we were well past, given everything we'd been through together.

Normally I also would have thrown in a few cutting reminders about just how many murderers, rapists, child molesters and other pillars of society I'd interviewed for him already.

Something about the way he said it diffused my anger though.

"I hear you," I said, giving him a mock salute.

As I did, I glanced at the guy on the other side of the one-way glass.

The suspect just sat there, a faint frown touching the edges of his dark lips.

For the first time however, he was staring at the one-way mirror.

It looked like he was staring directly at me.

Seeing the speckle of blood to the right of where that sharp mouth ended, I felt my pulse rise, in spite of myself.

21

Nick might just be right about this guy.

He usually was.

Pushing the thought out of my mind, I looked away from the glass, following Glen out into the corridor. As I did, I let my face slide into a blank, professional mask and hoped that this time it would protect me.

TWO
FIRST INTERVIEW

HE LOOKED ME OVER WHEN I WALKED IN.
Unlike a lot of people I'd interviewed in this room, suspects and witnesses alike, he didn't hide his appraisal. He also didn't do anything to try and get me on his side—like smile, or make his body language more accommodating or submissive.

He didn't try to intimidate me either, at least not that I noticed.

Again, the predominant emotion I saw in his assessment remained impatience.

He seemed, more than anything, to assume I was here to waste his time, too.

At the same time, I got the sense there was more there— more in relation to me specifically, I mean. Nothing sexual, at least I didn't think so.

What that "more" was exactly, I had absolutely no theories at that point.

Maybe I simply wasn't what—or who—he'd expected.

Maybe my appearance threw him.

I'm used to that, to a degree. I'm tall for a woman, almost

five-nine. My mom was Native American, like I said, and from one of the plains tribes that actually had some real height on them.

I'm not sure what our dad was, since I'd been young when our parents died and hadn't stayed in touch with any of his family... but he was tall too. I'd gotten hints of his bone structure, along with my mom's. I also got his light-hazel eyes, which people tell me are striking on me but were positively *riveting* on my father. My mom joked once she could have fallen in love with my father from his eyes alone.

The rest of me was my mother, according to my aunts. Straight black hair, full mouth, my sense of humor, even my curves, which were slightly less curvy from the martial arts classes, but not fully absent either.

In other words, even under all of my professional armor, I'm definitely female.

I can't exactly hide it, even in suits and with my hair tied tightly back.

For my part, I didn't bother to smile at him either, or do any of the usual heavy-handed shrink things to try and convince him I was "on his side" or even particularly friendly towards him. Right off, I got the feeling that those kinds of tactics wouldn't work on this guy.

He would see right through them.

Worse, trying it would probably cause him to dismiss me, too.

So yeah, I approached him assuming he was a psychopath.

Of course, the technical term these days, at least according to the latest Diagnostic and Statistical Manual of Mental Disorders, (or "DSM" as we shrink-types called it) is "Anti-Social Personality Disorder" or ASPD. Those of us who work in forensic psych

24

know a lot of the specific signs that go with this diagnosis—as well as ways to pick out the truly dangerous ones—but generally, there's a longer sussing-out period involved.

The most dangerous types were harder to spot.

Often highly intelligent, deeply manipulative, glibly charming, uninterested in other people and totally unwilling to acknowledge the individual rights of anyone apart from themselves, the more dangerous individuals with anti-social personality disorder were masters at evading detection by psychs who couldn't see past the veneer.

Narcissistic bordering on grandiose. Inflated sense of their own entitlement. Zero compunction about manipulating others. Generally lacking the capacity for love. Generally lacking the ability to feel shame or remorse. They either experienced only shallow emotions or feigned emotion altogether. They had a constant need for stimulation...

Well, you get the idea.

Truthfully, I doubted this guy would talk to me any more than he would talk to the cops.

Well, unless he decided I could help him in some way, or perhaps entertain him...since "short attention span" was often a big issue for the average psychopath.

Or perhaps he would treat me differently because he wanted a female audience instead of a male one; I was reasonably certain that only male cops had been tried on him so far.

Either way, I strongly suspected I wouldn't win him over by trying to play him for a fool, at least not right out of the gate.

I seated myself in the metal folding chair across the table from him.

I did my own quick once-over of the room, even though I'd been in here a few dozen times already—reminding myself of the location of the cameras, looking at the four corners out of habit. My eyes glanced down to where the suspect's ankles had been cuffed, not only to one another but to metal rings in the floor. His wrist cuffs were also chained to his waist, as well as to those same rings in the floor.

Glen already assured me that the range of the chains wouldn't allow him to reach me as long as I stayed in the chair.

Still, he'd warned me not to get any closer.

I didn't need to be told twice. The guy looked a lot bigger from in here.

He also looked significantly more muscular.

Leaning back in the hard, metal seat, I watched those gold, cat-like eyes flicker over me. They didn't pause anywhere for long, much less conduct one of those lecherous, lingering appraisals some convicts did in an attempt to unsettle me.

I sensed a methodicalness to his stare, instead.

That unnerved me a little, truthfully, maybe because it surprised me.

Even for a psychopath, that kind of focus was rare. Usually other people just weren't that interesting to them.

Then again, captivity may have changed that for him, too.

My eyes took in his appearance for the second time that day, lingering on the strangely high cheekbones still colored with smears of dried blood. I saw flakes of that blood on the surface of the table too, from where it had been rubbed off by his metal cuffs.

Wincing, I glanced up to find him staring at me once more, his gold eyes bordering on thoughtful as they took in my face.

When he didn't break the silence after a few seconds more, I leaned back more deliberately, crossing my legs in the dark-blue pantsuit I wore.

"So," I said, sighing. "You don't want to talk to anyone."

I didn't bother to state it as a question.

The man's eyes flickered back to my face, specifically to my eyes.

After a pause, I saw a faint smile tease the edges of his lips.

"I doubt my words would be very convincing," he said.

I must have jumped a little in my chair, but he pretended not to notice.

"...Covered in blood," he continued, motioning with one cuffed hand, likely as much as he could, given the restraints. Still, something in the odd grace of the gesture struck me, causing me to follow it with my eyes. "...Picked up near the scene of the crime. And you have witnesses, too, I suspect? Or did those three little girls decide it wasn't worth getting in trouble with their parents by calling the police in the wee hours of dawn?"

His words surprised me.

More, the longer he spoke.

Not only because he said them, but because they came out with a clipped, sharp accuracy and cadence. They wore the barest trace of an accent too, although it was one I couldn't identify. His manner of speech certainly implied a greater than average amount of education.

"In any case," the man said, leaning back so that the chains clanked at his ankles and on the table. "...I imagine I lack credibility, wouldn't you say, doc?"

I heard murmurings of surprise through my earpiece, too.

Apparently, I'd already gotten more out of him than any of them had.

I smoothed my expression without trying to hide my own surprise. Instead, I watched him openly, letting him see me do it.

"Doc," I said.

At his widening smile, I returned it, adding a touch of wry humor and raising an eyebrow.

"You think I am a doctor?"

"Aren't you?" he said at once. "Military, too, I suspect. Once upon a time. I saw you checking the corners. You've carried a gun...haven't you, doc? Maybe you even carry one now." He glanced around him ruefully. "Not in here, of course."

I shifted in my chair, not answering him.

"Aren't you a doctor?" he prompted.

"Depends on who you ask," I said drily, sighing a little.

Without taking my eyes off his, I leaned to the side somewhat, resting my arm on the back of the folding chair.

"Psychiatrist then," he said, adjusting his posture as well, a perhaps intentional replication of the old psychology trick of imitating the poses of those you want to confide in you.

"Or psychologist...only a real one, with a PhD. So perhaps it was a criminal psych ward where you honed your paranoia, not the military. You could be a social worker too, I suppose... although I have my doubts. You have too much of a clinical air about you, not enough of that needy, do-gooder type of saccharin that the softer arts tend to attract." His smile sharpened. "I would say dentist, but under the circumstances..."

Again that eloquent gesture of his fingers, this time indicating the room.

"...I am thinking that is not likely."

"I'm a psychologist," I told him easily. "Right in one."

"So you are here to assess me, then?" he said. "Or are they hoping the presence of an attractive female would send me frothing and panting? Get me to show my true colors? Shall I start screaming 'Die Bitch!' to satisfy those watching through the glass?"

I smiled again, unintentionally that time.

"If you want," I told him, muting the smile. "Do you want me to die?"

"Not particularly," he said.

"Really? Why not?" I said.

"I think you're the first person I've seen here with an IQ above that of a balding ape. Although that one inspector...he's got a *bit* of that base, instinctive kind of intellect. Only a bit, mind you. You know who I mean. Joe Handsome."

"It's Nick, actually," I said, smiling in spite of myself.

"Ah, he's a friend of yours, then?"

"Not a special friend, if that's what you mean."

"I didn't, but it's interesting information to have. Clearly the topic has come up between you, or you wouldn't have bothered to qualify it."

I shook my head, unimpressed with this last, and letting him see that, too.

"Really?" I said. "You're going there?"

"Going where?"

"Discredit the female by making some disparaging reference to her sexuality? Dismiss her as an equal by highlighting her value or lack thereof as a sexual object?"

"I profoundly apologize," he said, giving me a startled look. The surprise I could see in those almond eyes may have been mocking me, but it looked genuine.

"...My comments certainly weren't meant to be disparaging. I have no intention of resorting to such cheap tricks, doctor, simply to feel I've 'outwitted' you. Sadly, my ego won't permit it." Pausing, he added, "Would it help you to know I get sex on a regular basis too? I don't know that it would demean me in your eyes or if it would come off as bragging...in any case, I did not

29

bring up your own sexuality as anything other than a personal curiosity."

I tilted my head, still smiling, but letting my puzzlement show. "Why are you talking to me at all?" I asked finally.

"Why shouldn't I talk to you?" he said. "I've already told you that you're the first person to walk in here that I thought might be worth my attempting to communicate."

"Because I'm female?" I said.

"Because you seem to be less of a fool than the rest of them," he corrected me at once.

"But you said Nick had a mind?"

"I said he had a mind *of sorts*. Not the same thing at all. Although, given the nature of his intellect, he has undoubtedly chosen the right profession for himself."

I smiled again. "I'm sure that will be quite a relief for him."

I heard laughter in the earpiece that time, right before Nick spoke up.

"See if he'll tell you his name," he said to me.

"Certainly, if you really want to know," the suspect said, before I could voice the question aloud. "My name is Black. Quentin Black. Middle initial, R."

I stared at him, still recovering from the fact that he'd seemingly heard Nick give me an instruction through the earpiece.

Clearly, he wanted me to know he'd heard it, too.

"You heard that?" I said to him.

"Good ear, yes?" he said. Smiling, he gave me a more cryptic, yet borderline predatory look. "Less good with you, however. Significantly less good."

He paused, studying my face with eyes full of meaning.

I almost got the sense he was waiting for me to reply...or

maybe just to react. When I didn't, he leaned back in the chair, making another of those graceful, flowing gestures with his hand.

"I find that...fascinating, doc. Quite intriguing. Perhaps that is crossing a boundary with you again, however? To mention that?"

I paused on his words, then decided to dismiss them.

"Is that a real name?" I said. "Quentin Black. That doesn't sound real. It sounds fake."

"Real is all subjective, is it not?"

"So it's *not* real, then?"

"Depends on what you mean."

"Is it your *legal* name?"

"Again, depends on what you mean."

"I mean, could you look it up in a database and actually get a hit somewhere?"

"How would I know that?" he said, making an innocent gesture with his hands, again within the limits of the metal cuffs.

Realizing I wasn't going to get any more from him on that line of questioning, I changed direction. "What does the 'R' stand for?" I said.

"Rayne."

"Quentin Rayne Black?" I repeated back to him, still not hiding my disbelief.

"Would you believe me if I said my parents had a sense of whimsy?" he asked me.

"No," I said.

"Would you believe that I do, then?"

I snorted a laugh, in spite of myself. I heard it echoed through the earpiece, although I heard a few curses coming from that direction, too.

I shook my head at the suspect himself, but less in a "no" that time.

"Yes," I conceded finally. "So it *is* a made-up name, then?"

The man calling himself Quentin Black only returned my smile. His eyes once again looked shrewd, less thoughtful and more openly calculating.

Even so, his weird comment about "listening" came back to me.

Truthfully, he was looking at me as if he were listening very hard.

The thought made me slightly nervous.

Especially since I'd been doing the same to him from inside the observation booth.

Seeing the intelligence there, I found myself regrouping mentally as the silence stretched, reminding myself who and what I was dealing with. The fact that he'd nearly made me forget that in our back and forth of the last few moments was unnerving on its own.

I found myself looking him over deliberately, for the second time since I'd left the glass-enclosed booth behind the one-way mirror. I fought to reconcile his physical presence with the words I'd heard come out of that well-formed mouth. The two things, his physicality and his manner of speaking, didn't really fit at all, at least not from my previous experience in these kinds of interviews.

The all-black clothing, the dense, rock-like muscles I could see under that blood-soaked shirt, the expensive leather shoes, the expensive watch, the ethnically-ambiguous but somehow feral-looking face...nothing about him really fit, from his made-up name to his wryly humorous quipping with me.

I found myself staring at that strange, somehow *animal-*

evoking face with its abnormally high cheekbones and almond eyes, and wondered who in the hell this guy really was.

"Where are you from, Quentin?" I asked, voicing at least part of my puzzlement.

He shook his head though, that smile back to playing with the edges of his lips.

"You don't want to tell me that?" I said.

"No," he said. "...Clearly, I don't."

"What do you do for a living?" I said, trying again. "Do you have a job of some kind, Quentin? Some area of expertise you'd like to share?"

That time, he rolled his eyes openly.

Before I could respond to his obvious disdain, he let out an audible and impatient sigh.

"You're not going to resort to shrink games on *me* now, are you, doc?" he said, giving me another of those more penetrating stares. "...Not so soon in our new friendship? I haven't intimidated you already, have I?" At my silence, his voice grew bored. "The constant repetition of my given name. The clinical yet polite peppering of questions in an attempt to quietly undermine my sense of autonomy here..."

"Fine." I held up both of my palms in a gesture of surrender. "What do you want to talk about, Mr. Black? Do you want to tell me what you were doing at the Palace of Fine Arts earlier this morning?"

"Not here," he said cryptically, smiling at me again.

I frowned, glancing around the gunmetal gray room.

"Somewhere else, then?" I said.

"Yes," he said. "For all of your questions, doc. Including the ones I wouldn't answer before."

I gave him another puzzled smile. "I hate to tell you, Mr.

Black, but you're not likely to be anyplace that is significantly different from this room anytime soon. Not in terms of a non-institutional setting...if that's what you're driving at."

"It must certainly appear that way to you, yes," he said, raising his chained wrists for emphasis and glancing around the room with those gold eyes. "...But perhaps you are mistaken in that, doc. Perhaps you'll find that we can speak in a much more comfortable setting, just the two of us...and in not too long a time."

I narrowed my gaze at him.

It didn't sound like a threat, at least not coming from him. But the words themselves could definitely have been construed as one.

I gave him a wry smile. "You think so, huh?"

I do, a voice said clearly in my mind. *I do think so, doc.*

I jumped, violently.

Truthfully, I almost lost my balance in the chair.

"*Miri?*" Nick asked in my ear. "*Miri? Are you okay?*"

For a long-feeling few seconds I only stared at Black, breathing harder.

I could feel as much as see him watching me react. He smiled, lifting the bare corners of that sculpted mouth. Then he shrugged, his expression smoothing.

"Perhaps you'll accept a raincheck on that particular discussion, doc?" he said. "...After I've finished my business here?"

It unnerved me, hearing him use the nickname yet again. I knew it wasn't exactly an original thing to call someone in my line of work, but it still struck me as deliberate.

I fought the other thing out of my mind, sure I must have imagined it.

34

Even so, the smile on my face grew strained.

"Okay," I said. "You pick the topic, then. For today I mean... pre-raincheck."

Quentin Black smiled, leaning back deliberately in the bolted, metal chair.

"No," he said, after assessing me again with those strangely animal eyes. "No, I think we're done for now, doc. It was my *very* great pleasure to meet you, however."

I pursed my lips. "You don't want to talk to me anymore?" I said.

I want to talk to you so badly I can fucking taste it, that same voice said in my mind, making me jump again, but less violently that time. My breath stopped, locking in my chest as the voice rose even more clearly. *But not here, doc. Not here. Patience. And believe me when I say I am speaking to myself in this, even more than I am to you...*

I could only sit there, breathing, staring at him.

Those gold eyes never wavered.

When I didn't move after a few more seconds, or speak, he smiled.

Do they know what you are, doc? Does that handsome cop in the next room have any idea why it is that you are so very, very good at your job? Or how you managed to keep him alive that time in Afghanistan...?

My chest clenched more.

It hurt now, like a fist had reached inside me, squeezing my heart.

The voice fell silent.

The man in front of me looked at me, his expression close to expectant. Then he gazed pointedly down at my engagement ring.

Does anyone know about you, doc? Anyone at all?

My throat closed as he raised his eyes back to mine.

Those gold flecked irises studied my face, watching my reaction.

I can't hear you, the voice said next, flickering with a tinge of frustration. *I cannot hear you at all...but I know from your face that you hear me, doc. That shield of yours is damned strong. I confess, it's positively turning me on at this point...but it also makes me very curious. Were you ever ranked, sister? If so, I would love to know at what level...*

Another smile ghosted his lips, even as a curl of heat slid through my lower abdomen, one that didn't feel like it originated from me, at least not entirely.

It made my face flush hot, even as my thighs clenched together in reflex.

I'll show you mine, if you show me yours... the voice said, softer.

My throat tightened, choking me with a caught swallow.

Still, he didn't say anything aloud.

We'll talk more later, doc, I heard in my mind, softer still. *I have so many, many questions. So many things I'd like to discuss. But I really do not wish to do any of that here...not with them watching us. They are wondering at this silence as it is. You must try to speak to me again, doc, before your handsome cop decides there is a problem. Before he and his meat-headed partner make an issue of it...*

I blinked again, my heart now slamming against my ribs. But he wasn't looking at me now.

As I watched, Quentin Rayne Black lapsed back into the bored, stone-faced man I'd glimpsed through the window before I'd entered the room.

I'd finally managed to clear my throat.

Clenching my hands together in my lap, conscious of how

clammy they felt, I kept my voice carefully polite. "Do you want to tell me about the body in the park, Mr. Black?" I said.

Nothing. Silence.

"Mr. Black?" I said, hearing the slight tremble in my voice. "Did you kill that woman? Did you pose her in that wedding dress?"

He didn't look up from where he stared down between his cuffed hands.

I tried again, asking the same thing a few different ways.

But nothing I said in those next fifteen or so minutes appeared to reach him. I tried being friendly, annoying, disdainful, mocking. I belittled his intellect...even threw out a few offers to deal, along with some not-so-veiled threats. Nothing.

I got nothing.

In fact, I doubt I penetrated the veneer of that thoughtful, somehow puzzle-solving stare he aimed at the empty surface of the metal table.

Clearly, I'd been dismissed.

THREE
A GUT FEELING

I RETREATED FROM THE ROOM AFTER I'D BEEN INSIDE LESS THAN thirty minutes.

I honestly had no idea how to feel about what had just happened.

Fear kind of ran over all of the other reactions I might have had.

Fear for my own sanity. Fear of him...maybe even terror of him.

Fear of what he'd done...what I was having increasing difficulty convincing myself had only been some kind of auditory hallucination. Fear around the sinking feeling I had that Quentin Black's mention of being locked up in the police station only "temporarily" hadn't just been idle bragging. I didn't think his confidence on that point stemmed from normal, sociopathic delusion, either...which is how the cops listening would have heard it.

It's likely how I would have heard it too, if that's *all* I'd heard. But how could I possibly warn the others?

Quentin Black must have known I *wouldn't* be able to warn them.

Despite everything running through my head, some part of me almost forgot that the police watching our interview missed a good portion of my exchange with Black. Therefore, when I knocked on the interrogation room door and it opened to Nick and Glen standing there in the hallway, I was shocked to see the blatant smiles in both of their eyes.

They didn't say anything aloud until they'd closed the door on Black, of course.

They didn't even crack real smiles until then.

Once the door *had* closed, however, Nick grinned openly, slapping me on the back with one hand. "See?" he told Glen in a gloating kind of voice. "What did I tell you?"

I gave him an eye roll, fighting to keep my expression blank as I combed fingers through my hair. Glancing back at the closed door, I tried to shove Mr. Quentin Black out of my mind, at least well enough to act normal for the next few minutes until my heart stopped pounding like a damned jackhammer.

I gratefully accepted a cup of fresh coffee handed to me by Angel Deveraux, another homicide inspector who worked the Northern District. The coffee cup's paper jacket proclaimed it as being from The Royale Blend, which only sharpened my gratitude.

Glad of the distraction if nothing else, I grinned at her. "You're not fetching coffee for these bozos now, are you?" I asked, taking a sip as I quirked an eyebrow.

Angel Deveraux gave a derisive snort.

A buffed, black, ex-beat cop from one of the roughest parts of the city, Angel had stunning light brown eyes and a prominent jaw on a sharply beautiful face. Angel and I went to the same martial arts classes as Nick, and often got thrust together as sparring partners since we were roughly the same height and weight, even though Angel was a few belts above me. She usually kicked my ass, but I learned a ton from her, so I didn't really mind.

Angel had known Nick even longer than I had.

They grew up in the same neighborhood near Hunter's Point.

Maybe because of that, they often bickered more like family members than friends.

"No," Angel said, giving Nick a pointed look, as if the comment had come from him and not me. "It's just that *some* of us have a little thing called manners." She smiled at me. "Truthfully, I didn't even know you were here, doc. I called up from the coffee line at Royale, knowing these jokers didn't get a lot of sleep last night and might be slumped drooling over their desks. Instead I find them up here, giggling like little boys as they watch you make the only progress we've had all day with our exciting new serial killer..."

"Technically, he's not a serial killer yet," I informed her.

"He's killed seven now," she told me, daring me with her eyes to disagree.

"Seven people," I conceded. "Two incidents. Still only a killer...technically."

"Technically, my ass," she snorted. "What about the wedding theme?"

"A weird killer," I corrected. "Make that an *alleged,* weird killer...still not a serial killer, or even an alleged serial killer, not until he hits magic number three. You might be able to make a strong argument for a spree killer, though. Depending on motive."

Angel rolled her eyes, aiming a thumb at me while she shook her head at Nick and Glen.

41

"Get a load of doc here, all hoity-toity now that she got Mr. Quentin Black to give her a fake name and play his little head games with her for a spell."

I laughed as I started to follow the three of them back down the florescent-lit corridor with its lime-green tile.

"Fair enough," I conceded, grinning as I took another sip of the scalding hot coffee. "Still sounds like a solid point for the head-shrinker and a big, fat zero for the fuzz."

Angel snorted a laugh, shaking her head as she glanced back at me.

"Drink your coffee, doc," she advised, waving over her shoulder at me with one hand, her tone mocking. "You best keep that smart mouth of yours busy for a little while, or we might have to drum up some charges against you...especially since from what I heard, it sounded like your *serial killer...*" She emphasized the words. "...Maybe has a bit of a crush on you."

"Who doesn't?" Nick said, winking at me.

Glen laughed, giving me an over-the-shoulder smile, too.

I fought to keep the smile on my face, couldn't that time.

Instead I sipped more coffee to cover it.

By then we were all back inside the glass-enclosed observation room, standing and leaning by the two tables that filled the rectangular space. The room had the dark, bluish cast of an aquarium, with the only window aiming into the interrogation room itself.

I found myself putting my back decisively to the view of Quentin Black.

"Did you just come from the scene?" I asked Angel.

She nodded, hands on her hips. She leaned on the edge of a table shoved up against the back wall. "Yeah," she said, sighing. "You're glad you missed that one, doc."

42

"Where's the body now?" I said, looking at Nick and then back to Angel. "Does the coroner's office have it yet?"

Nick gave me a surprised look. I didn't usually ask him for details like that. Not when it came to that end of the forensics.

"Yeah," he said. He had a coffee of his own I noticed. He pulled it off the same low table where I leaned my butt, then sat on one of the two folding chairs, looking up at me. "Why?"

"I thought I might look at it," I said. "The body. You know. Get an idea of the m.o."

Angel gave me a look that time, too. She glanced at Nick and Glen. She didn't say anything though.

"Sure thing, doc," Nick said, his shrug a little too studied. "Anything you want."

"Is it *that* weird I'd want to see it?" I said, smiling a little.

"It's a little weird," Glen volunteered. "You hate blood, doc."

Grimacing a little, I nodded, then looked back at Nick. "You're running that name, right?" I pressed. "The Quentin Black one?"

"Sure. I sent it over as soon as he said it," Nick said. That puzzlement leaked to his voice.

I watched the three of them exchange another look, right as Glen cleared his throat.

"You okay, doc?" Nick said then. "That guy rattle you?"

Looking around at the three of them, I realized they were all watching me now, their cop faces on higher alert. Some of them were doing a better job of hiding it than others. Letting out a sigh, I combed my fingers through my hair again.

"Yeah," I admitted. "Maybe."

"You did so well in there," Nick said. "I would have never known."

43

"You were a real pro," Glen seconded, leaning against the same table as me and folding his massive arms before he gave me a sympathetic smile.

Angel said nothing.

Looking between the three of them again, I exhaled in annoyance. "I'm fine, okay? It's just...you know. There's something about him."

"Yeah," Nick snorted, anger leaking into his words. "He's a murdering nutcase." Looking at me more carefully then, he said, "Well? What kind of nutcase is he, Miri? You going to tell us? Or is it a secret?"

He had his cop voice on again.

I realized he was right.

We hadn't gone through the whole "brain-picking" part of this exercise, where they asked me questions about what I thought of the suspect and what he might do.

I wished I could just skip it for this one.

I really didn't want to do a psychological profile on Quentin Black. Not until I had a much better idea of what the hell just happened in there. Truthfully, I felt like I'd just be throwing darts at this point. Or lying to them in a sense, giving them the book stuff when I wasn't sure I believed it. But I also knew Nick wouldn't let me off the hook so easily.

It was, after all, why he'd brought me here.

Glancing over my shoulder in spite of myself, I gazed through the window at the man sitting inside the interrogation room.

I flinched a little when I saw him staring back at me through the one-way glass.

Once again, I could almost imagine him seeing me in here.

"Okay," I said, exhaling in an irritated-sounding sigh. I

looked away from the window, folding my arms. "But not here. We should go somewhere else."

Nick's eyes flickered in surprise, right before he glanced at the one-way mirror himself. I practically felt the question on him as he frowned in the direction of Quentin Black. Despite his cautioning me earlier, I'd never reacted to a suspect like this.

Nick knew that, as well as I did.

"Why?" he said finally, his voice openly wary as he looked back at me. Seeing my arched eyebrow, he frowned. "We always debrief in here."

He was right of course. We did always debrief in here.

Still, the feeling that we'd be overheard if we stayed here — or, more specifically, that the three cops would be overheard — persisted.

The feeling was strong enough that I dug in my heels.

"We should go downstairs, Nick," I said, my voice firm. "I think better in natural light. And I need more sugar for my coffee anyway," I lied. "Besides, I don't think we're going to learn any more by taking turns staring at Mr. Black."

Angel laughed at my words. Glen smiled, too.

Nick didn't.

I also didn't miss the questioning glances I got from all three of them, although Angel did better with hiding hers than the other two.

I didn't take sugar in my coffee.

Angel and Nick knew that, at least. I had no idea if Glen knew my coffee quirks or not.

Even so, when I motioned towards the door a second time, they all rose to their feet and shuffled out, walking in the direction of the elevators along with me.

I couldn't help wondering if Quentin R. Black felt us go.

I DIDN'T END UP TELLING THEM MUCH.

I knew it frustrated Nick especially, probably more so that I made them change venues just to tell them jack squat. It frustrated him enough that he offered to go with me to the morgue, likely to see if he could pull more details out of me while I looked over the body.

I knew he was still puzzled by the morgue request too.

Usually I only looked at the body if they hadn't caught the perp yet. Meaning, if I was trying to give them a profile based on the crime scene versus having a real-life human being to assess. When they had an actual suspect in custody, I often just looked over the paper. They were pretty thorough with the documentation these days and I wasn't a medical examiner, so seeing the forensics assessments was more valuable for me anyway.

Most of the time, seeing the body in person wasn't going to help me do my job.

Nick had me go with him to the coroner a few times in cases like this anyway, when he thought it might help me get a better handle on a suspect or victim. But it usually caused a fair bit of groaning on my part, and I don't think I'd ever *asked* to go before.

Part of that was the war, I knew.

A probably bigger part of it was, I still couldn't help associating the morgue with Zoe, even after all these years. The first time I'd ever been inside one of these cold, chemical-smelling rooms was when I got called in to ID my sixteen-year-old sister.

By then, our parents were already dead, so I was the only one left to do it.

I'd been eighteen. Just old enough to make the cut.

Not long after that, maybe only a few months later, I joined the military. The military paid for my undergraduate degree. Scholarships and loans paid for the rest. And before I got my degree, while I was in the Middle East, I met Nick.

My life kind of went where it went after that.

No regrets. No looking back.

Even so, I'd never really recovered from Zoe's death. It hit me harder than the death of my parents somehow, although I couldn't have said why exactly. Truthfully, I think I was pretty numb for the first few years after I saw her lying on a slab in a room a lot like this one.

I couldn't help flashing to that experience now, as I stood over a different stainless steel table with yet another young girl lying dead and naked on top of it.

This time, it was easier to keep that professional veneer, if only because I could feel Nick's eyes watching me every second we spent in that windowless room.

Nick knew I hated this stuff. He'd joked that it was funny I never got squeamish during the war but put the body in a sterile room and cover it with a sheet and I acted like I was afraid the damned thing might rise from the dead and try to kill me.

He was right. I hated these cold, dead-feeling rooms.

I'd never liked gore in wartime either, although he was right—I could push past it to do the job.

It just wasn't my thing, to rubber-neck any part of the more violent aspects of life. To me there's something deeply disrespectful about looking for any reason other than an absolute necessity to do my work. But now I stood over a strange young woman's body while the coroner explained to me and Nick how she'd been murdered.

"So these cuts that were done for purely cosmetic purposes," I said, interrupting him again. "...You're sure they had nothing to do with either killing her, or anything that could be construed as part of a struggle?"

The coroner nodded, looking up at me.

His gaze sharpened on my face.

I had that affect on some of the older guys.

I think how I looked maybe bothered some of them. Or possibly my sex...or my age, even though I'm thirty years old. Or maybe it was the lack of scientific letters after my name. Or how blunt I could be.

Whatever it was, they never expected me to clinical-speak them, or say things without a nervous question mark at the end. They also never seemed to expect me to have a brain, and seemed deeply suspicious of me once they realized I did have one.

"I don't know about 'cosmetic,'" he said, his voice gruff. He sniffed in some emotion I didn't bother to pin down. "But," he conceded more grudgingly. "You're correct in that the evidence doesn't suggest an immediate reason for some of her non-fatal injuries, and at least one of them appears to have some meaning. In fact, quite a few of them are post-mortem...so the possibility that he did them for more psychological reasons presents a reasonable theory, even apart from the symbol we found."

He hit the word *theory* a tad hard, I noticed.

I ignored that too, nodding.

I found myself lost in thought, staring down at the cuts along the ribs and belly of the dead girl. Mostly, though, I found myself staring at the symbol the coroner had just referenced. A series of three spirals, it mirrored the same exact symbol Nick showed me just a week before on the bodies of all of the victims found at Grace Cathedral. About the size of my palm, it had been carved in the same place on all of the victims as well, right in the middle of their chests, almost like some kind of chakra or ancient heart symbol.

"This one happened while she was still alive though... right?" I said.

"Correct," the coroner said. "Same as with the other victim. Since the design is perfectly symmetrical and the exact same size in every case, we think he used a custom-made implement to leave the mark. Probably made of something like razor blades... or a scalpel. Roughly that type of edge. It's too fine to have been done with most knives."

I nodded, still staring down at the precise cuts.

Nick's voice startled me out of my trance, bringing my eyes sharply up to his.

"Any theories on why that's important, doc?" he said softly. "Related to today, I mean?"

The coroner gave him an annoyed look.

I wanted to laugh when I realized he was offended Nick was implying I was a real doctor.

I didn't though. Laugh, that is.

I shook my head. "Not really. Not yet."

"Liar," he chided, softer. He gave the coroner a brief glance before leaning closer to murmur in my ear. "You're hiding something from me, Miri... I want to know what. And why."

I rolled my eyes, giving him an irritated look. "Hardly," I said.

"Then you're not sharing something," he rephrased, speaking in his normal tone of voice. "...Which is the same thing. You've got something you're following here. Spill it."

Sighing, I smoothed my hair with the back of my wrist to avoid touching it with the gloves. I'd put it into a ponytail to come in here. Glancing between Nick and the coroner, I thought for a minute more, then more or less told them both the truth.

"That man you had me talk to," I said, aiming my words at Nick. "The one calling himself Quentin Black. There's something about his personality that doesn't mesh with this. With the way the murder took place, I mean."

Nick frowned. I could tell he hated this theory already.

All he said was, "Go on."

I shrugged, throwing up a hand. "There is no 'go on.' Not at this point."

"You have *something*, doc. Why do you think that?"

"It's nothing substantial. I'd prefer to wait."

"I'd prefer if you didn't."

Sighing, I gave him another look. Then I gave in.

"All right," I said, turning slightly to face him. "The man I met today didn't strike me as theatrical, Nick. Not in any way. Quite the contrary. He's hyper-practical. Goal-oriented. Not a time-waster. It feeds into his narcissism, I suspect...or self-importance, at least. He views his time as infinitely too valuable to spend on anything not directly related to his immediate ends. I suspect he views his time as worth significantly more than that of most people...and his goals as more important certainly. Perhaps even 'save the world' important. Certainly well beyond the comprehension of the vast majority of us mere mortals..."

"But not you," Nick said, studying my eyes.

I rolled my eyes. "Oh, I'm sure I make the list too. He was entertaining himself with me. But I wouldn't say that put me at his 'level,' in his eyes."

Seeing Nick frown, clearly disagreeing, I shrugged.

"...Anyway, if I'm right, the profile doesn't fit," I said, my voice carefully flat. "While I would *definitely* believe him capable of murder, I don't see him cutting up a girl for fun...much less dressing her in a wedding outfit and posing her the way this one did. That implies passion. Eroticism of some kind. Revenge at least, or some form of sadism...even religious fervor possibly, given the odd symbol and its placement. Black might be a sociopath...and he's likely a narcissist. But I don't think he'd..."

I paused, still thinking aloud as I waved a hand over the body of the dead girl.

"...*Lower* himself to playing with his food. Understand?"

"No," Nick said. He shifted his weight on his feet, folding his arms. "No, I don't understand. What the hell are you talking about, Miri?"

I sighed. "I said it was just a theory."

"What makes you think the whole 'ritual' of this isn't part of Black's goals?" Nick said, which told me he'd been listening to me at least. "You said he wouldn't waste time on something not a part of his whole 'thing,' right? What if this *is* his thing, Miri? What if it means something to him? Something we just don't understand yet?"

I met his gaze over the body of the dead girl, then shrugged.

"It's possible," I conceded.

"Possible? But you still don't think so?"

"No. Not without evidence to actually *suggest* that, Nick."

"Why not?" he said, his voice openly frustrated. "You aren't even going to entertain that idea a little bit, are you, doc?"

Looking back down at the girl, I found myself focusing on the heavy coating of make-up on her face, all the way down to her neckline.

It must have taken time to apply.

51

There was so much of it, and it was so flawlessly smooth on her cheeks and forehead and around her eyes, it made her look like a porcelain doll. Or really, paradoxically, like a child. It wasn't sexy make-up, by any means. Rather, it seemed to age her downwards, implying a kind of flawless beauty more associated with pre-pubescence.

The only thing breaking the illusion was the few spots of blood that made it above her neck, and the smear on her throat which probably happened when they moved her. Still staring down at her face, feeling a sudden pain in my chest as I realized how young she was in reality, I shrugged. Her true age had been partly obscured by the half-inch of foundation and blush and powder, as well.

She couldn't be more than twenty-five.

"I'm not ruling anything out," I said.

"You sure about that, Miri?"

The sharpness in his voice caused me to lift my eyes a second time. When I spoke next, my clinical voice had more bite.

"Reasonably sure," I said, leveling my stare. "But I'm not going to spend a lot of time on leads that *you* like simply because you're too attached to your current suspect, Nick. Especially when I can tell your emotions are coloring your view of him."

Nick made a disbelieving sound. "*My* emotions?" he said. "Coloring *my* view, doc? You sure that's what's going on?"

"You asked for my opinion," I said coldly. "My *clinical* opinion."

"And is that what I'm getting?" he said.

I blinked at him.

I glanced at the coroner, who was watching and listening to the two of us. He pushed his dark-rimmed glasses up his nose before he re-folded his arms, smirking at me. Seeing the smug

52

look behind those thick lenses, I focused back on Nick, deciding to ignore it.

Guy was obviously kind of a prick.

"I'm just not sure it's his style, Nick," I said, letting some of the cooler, more clinical tone drop from my voice. I decided to be more honest, talk to him more as my friend. "I can't explain that fully yet, which is why I wasn't trying...but I strongly suspect you might need to at least look for a possible accomplice. If you hadn't pushed me, I would have waited until I had something more *concrete* in that regard, okay? As it is, you're just going to have to trust me that I'm looking at this objectively. Or pull me off the case and find another forensic psychologist."

There was a silence.

I'd been trying to crack through that more suspicious thing of Nick's, to hit him with sincerity in an attempt to get him to lower his guard.

When I studied the gaze of Homicide Detective Naoko Tanaka through that silence however, I found myself thinking that I'd taken the wrong approach.

In fact, my words had the exact opposite effect from what I'd hoped. A warier look had risen in the background of his stare. I also saw the cop veneer harden over his expression, and the more concentrated scrutiny he aimed at me as a part of that.

He thought I was managing him.

He thought I was using my intellect and training to snow him into backing off.

Hell, he might even be right.

Moreover, I got a glimmer of exactly what lay behind his sudden re-appraisal of me.

Realizing as I did that my "glimmer" might have been exactly what Mr. Quentin Black had been accusing me of inside

53

that interrogation room, I shut that down, too, but not before the memory of our exchange heated my face.

Unfortunately, Nick saw that, too.

He also took my sudden blush in decidedly the wrong way.

I could feel it...even though I didn't want to.

Then again, I'd always been able to feel a lot more than I really wanted to.

FOUR
OFF THE CASE

I GUESS IT'S TIME FOR A CONFESSION FROM ME.

It's not the easiest thing in the world for me to admit, but for the sake of full disclosure...I already knew there was something different about me.

Before Quentin Black, I mean.

One way to put it might be this: ever since I was a kid, I'd known things that most people didn't know. Things a lot of people would argue I *couldn't* know.

Things others would say I *shouldn't* know.

When I was a kid, the tough part wasn't figuring out that I knew those things. The hard part—the part that caused me the most confusion and loneliness and grief—was figuring out that most people *didn't* know those things.

Thank God I had my sister Zoe.

Maybe that's why I missed her so much now. She'd been like me, too. We practically had our own language growing up, since it was through her as much as on my own that I realized how "different" we were from other kids.

Even so, I was the oldest, so I learned a lot of those lessons first. Like, for example, how mentioning anything I heard or saw in other people's minds would get me a lot of blank stares, cocked eyebrows, deafening silences...and fear.

Mostly fear.

Including from our own parents.

I learned to keep my mouth shut about what I could feel, sense...and yes, sometimes hear...off the minds of people around me. I taught Zoe the same, once I knew she was like me. It was a survival skill we both learned young.

Moreover, it wasn't enough to simply not mention that we could hear and see those things. We also had to be extremely careful not to *act* on the things we knew, at least those things where a reasonable explanation couldn't be found for how we knew them. We had to be extremely careful not to change our behavior in incriminating ways.

Sometimes that was really, really hard to do.

It got a lot harder after Zoe died.

It also got a lot more lonely.

Psychology was a logical choice for me in school, for that reason alone. If I could figure out how regular people worked, I'd be able to fit in with them easier. It's also why I would have preferred doing pure research, as opposed to getting paid to sit and listen to people lie to me all day while I had to smile and nod politely and pretend not to notice.

I hated even the *word* "psychic," much less all the New Agey crap associated with it.

But yeah, I guess it fits.

I, Miriam Kimi Fox, am a psychic.

Truthfully, the thought gives me hives.

It was a lot easier to bear when Zoe and I could joke about it. Since Zoe died, I'd run into other so-called "psychics" over the years too, of course.

Fortunately, most of them had absolutely no idea what I was.

In fact, before Quentin Black, I only remember one woman who stared at me particularly hard, then asked me what the hell I was doing with my mind. She complained that she couldn't read a damned thing off me. She was an older woman, kind of witchy in terms of her clothes and her long braided gray hair and all the crystals she wore.

She was also really blunt.

She told me there was something very different about me. She also said, somewhat accusingly as I recall, that all she saw around me was a bunch of "smokescreen bullshit" I'd put up to hide my mind from anyone who might be looking.

She was right, of course.

Because the thing with being a mind-reader is this: even if you sort of know no one else can probably do it, the fact that *you* can do it makes you paranoid. When I was a kid, especially—before I figured out that those voices and pictures and whispers of emotion didn't register for the vast majority of normal people—I pretty much assumed any thought I had, I might as well be shouting it in a crowded room.

Since Zoe could hear me, it seemed logical that others could, too.

Perhaps obviously, as a result, being psychic also makes you careful about what you think.

The truth is, you stay paranoid to some degree, even after you figure out that it's unlikely anyone else will hear you. You still wonder. It still crosses your mind. Like speaking a foreign language around people from another country, you still hesitate now and then, wondering if maybe they *do* understand you. One or two of them, anyway.

After all, *you* can.

It stands to reason that others must be able to hear you, too.

Totally opposite to me, most of those other "psychics" I encountered wore their psychic creds loud and proud. Some even made a living at it, hanging the standard glowy handprint on storefront windows and scattering eagle feathers and crystal balls and Buddha statues around their incense-filled caves beyond a purple-curtained door.

Some even worked with the cops like me, although not exactly in the same capacity. None of the ones I ran into had much more than a low-level ability, though. At least not apart from the witchy woman who glimpsed the edges of my shield, and I'd never managed to find her again after that one time we crossed paths.

Some were out-and-out scammers.

I never told anyone but Zoe what I could do. I lived in San Francisco though, so I couldn't avoid the psychic thing entirely. The yuppie-tech takeover was almost complete at that point, but San Francisco still had the remnants of its New Age hippy culture, especially in some parts of town. So I just ignored it. Played normal.

I was able to ignore it too...the vast majority of the time.

No one could see me. Which was just fine with me.

Another big advantage to having an ability that pretty much no one else has? No one else has any way of knowing *you* have that ability either.

Well, as long as you keep your mouth shut and act like everyone else.

H EY, MIRI."
I looked up, frowning a bit from behind the bluish glow of my laptop screen.

It was the next morning.

Early, like it had been that first day.

Early enough that I was tired, even though I'd at least finished my first cup of coffee. Ian was out of town for work so I'd spent the night alone, which maybe didn't help. Even though Ian and I still had our own places, we shared a fair bit of closet space and I usually slept at his house in China Beach when he was in town.

Ian and I fought again the night before too...on the phone that is, and mostly about how much he was gone. Now I felt guilty about the argument, in addition to everything else. When I'd woken up about three hours before my alarm went off, I hadn't been able to get back to sleep, despite working myself hard in sparring class the night before.

Pushing my laptop away from me a little bit, I folded my hands on the top of my desk, quirking an eyebrow at Nick, who stood in the doorway, looking a bit sheepish where he held two large cups of coffee from the Royale Blend.

I didn't fully buy the "aw shucks" look on his face, but I noted it.

He'd decided to take this approach. I got why he was going this way, but I could clearly see the cop watching me from behind that stare.

I also knew exactly why he was here.

"So," he said carefully, still lingering by the door. "I think I really do need to boot you off the case, Miri. The wedding one."

I let out a humorless sound, folding my arms.

Feigning surprise, I smiled at him.

"Oh?" I said only. "How did I get off so easy? You know my birthday's not for a few more months yet, right?"

There was a silence.

Then Nick grinned. That time, the relief in his eyes looked and felt a lot more genuine.

He walked over to me at once, plopping one of the coffee cups he carried on my desk next to the laptop before he dumped his muscular bulk into the worn chair that squatted across from my desk. I watched him relax into the dark red leather as it squeaked against his leather-jacketed shoulders.

"I decided to take pity on you," Nick grinned, after he took off the plastic hood of his coffee cup and balanced the cup between his thighs.

I watched him produce two packets of sugar from the pocket of his jacket and rip off the tops before dumping them into the black coffee.

Coffee was the only time Nick allowed himself sugar.

He was kind of a health nut in most other respects.

"...You've clearly got the hots for our clown," he added, glancing up with a wink as he leaned over to toss the empty sugar packets into my trash bin. "I didn't want you getting all teary-eyed when they gas his ass at Quentin." Raising his cup in a mock toast without its plastic lid, he added, "Quentin at Quentin...poetic, don't you think?"

I knew he was referring to the local federal prison, San Quentin, which was just on the other side of the Golden Gate Bridge.

"Cute," I said, giving him a wry smile and leaning back in my own chair. I picked up the cup he'd brought me, smelling it before I took a grateful sip. Smiling when I lowered it, I met his gaze, watching him look at me with that smile still ghosting his face.

"Are you going to tell me the real reason you don't want me on it, Nick? You got some new hot-shot psych student whose pants you're trying to inspect?"

He let out a snort of laughter, involuntarily I think.

He nearly coughed out coffee through his nose in the process.

Relief wafted off him tangibly that time, even more than before.

That relief made me relax, too.

I saw his face grow serious, even as he dropped the act he'd used to come in here.

"The guy's too interested in you, Miri. Way too interested. Frankly, I don't want him getting another look at you...much less talking to you on a regular basis." He hesitated, then gave me a more openly apologetic look. "Especially since we might have to cut him loose for awhile...temporarily, I mean."

I stiffened. "Cut him loose?"

"Yeah. Maybe even later today." He gave me another apologetic look, but that one had more steel behind it. "*Temporarily*, like I said. We just need a little more time."

"Why?" I couldn't keep the bewilderment out of my voice.

Moreover, my heart was already pounding, remembering how confident Black had been on that point when I'd talked to him in the interview room.

"Fucker lawyered up," Nick said with a shrug. "He's got a good one, too."

"Who?" I knew most of the defense attorneys in town. The good ones anyway.

"Farraday," Nick said. "You heard of him? Guy's out of New York...a real ball buster. Made his name in that dual homicide mess with that investment shit-heel a few years back. The one with the crow bar. Remember?"

I nodded. I remembered.

My lips firmed as I still fought puzzlement.

"With the bad toupee, right?" I said, taking another sip of coffee. When Nick grunted a laugh, nodding, I cleared my throat. "I thought he mostly worked for Wall Streeters. How the hell is Black affording him?"

Hesitating another half-second, Nick put his coffee down on the edge of my desk, fishing around in the pocket of his beat-up leather jacket—the opposite pocket from the one where he got his sugar packets. Leaning back over my desk, he tossed something at me, what looked like a rectangular business card. Leaning back in the same motion, he grabbed his coffee cup on the way back to the leather chair. The chair let out a protesting squeak when the two sets of leathers rubbed together a second time.

"Asshole's a P.I.," Nick grunted. "Can you believe it?"

I gave him a blank look. "Who?"

"Black. Quentin Black. He's a P.I. Licensed and everything."

"He's a P.I.?" My jaw dropped.

Looking down, I snatched up the business card he'd tossed me.

Nick nodded grimly, watching me look at it. "Rich as fuck, too. Doesn't even need to work, he's got so much money...at least if the reports are right. Once Farraday showed, your Mr. Black started singing a different song altogether. *Now* he claims he was at the scene on a case. Says he stayed silent to 'await legal advice' because he knew that circumstantially it looked bad for him. Says he was afraid of jail, afraid he'd say the wrong thing."

Nick let out an annoyed snort to let me know what he thought of *that* story.

I was still staring down at the card.

Somehow, the damned thing *felt* like him...like I could feel some remnant of Quentin Black's fingertips imprinted on the linen stock.

The card itself was bone white but for a black eagle symbol stamped in the center. The symbol looked almost military, with Quentin Black's initials worked into the design at the bottom in an archaic-looking script.

Flipping over the card, I found a website address as well as a physical one on California Street. The street number was low enough that it had to be near the water. That placed Mr. Quentin Black's business offices in some of the most expensive real estate in the world.

His office was on the forty-eighth floor.

I couldn't even imagine what kind of rent that must be.

I cleared my throat, keeping the disinterested look on my face with an effort.

"How did he explain the blood?" I said, my voice neutral. "He was covered in blood. Did his lawyer have anything on that?"

When I glanced up, Nick scowled.

"He claims he was trying to 'save' her," Nick grunted. "That she was still alive when he got there...barely. He's not disputing he was there...or that the blood is hers. He says he tried to put pressure on some of the worst cuts to stop the bleeding."

"What did the coroner say?"

Nick shrugged. "He says it's possible."

"Possible?" I frowned. "Likely-possible? Or unlikely-possible?"

"Possible," Nick said, giving me a harder stare. "Why? You still think he didn't do it, Miri? Because it's too 'theatrical' for him or whatever?"

I nodded, but not really in answer to his question.

"So?" I said. "Will his story hold up? In court."

Nick's scowl deepened. "With his lawyer? Probably. Fucker's a licensed P.I. We've got zilch on motive. He's got an alibi for the Grace Cathedral thing...including a plane ticket showing he was out of the country. We ran his creds and they're all up to date. Further, he told us last night that the family of Esther Velaquez hired him a few weeks ago. Now we have to run that down, too, see if we can match it to his story about the Palace killing."

I nodded, watching his face cautiously.

Esther Velaquez was the primary victim of the first wedding murder. They found her just like this one, with a few inches of make-up on her face and posed in an expensive wedding dress almost like a ballerina. Only she hadn't been alone. Rather, she'd bled to death inside Grace Cathedral along with five of her wedding party — three bridesmaids and two groomsmen. By far most of the damage in terms of cutting had been done to her, though.

The wedding hadn't even been scheduled for two months.

All of them had that same spiral symbol cut into their chests. The killer only did it to her while she'd still been alive, however. The rest got it post-mortem.

The story was heartbreaking really. The six of them had gone out to dinner and then to a bar to celebrate. They all left the bar together and no one ever saw them alive again.

By all accounts, Esther had been a kind person, with a lot of friends and family.

The cops speculated that the wedding party might have gone to the cathedral in some connection to the wedding itself, but no one really knew for sure how they'd gotten there. After the Palace killing, it looked less likely that they'd gone willingly.

"How did he explain that he was at the scene at all?" I said, still thinking aloud. "Black. Did he claim to have followed a suspect there?"

Nick's scowl deepened. "No. He says he and his staff staked out various locations around town, in the hopes of catching the killer in the act. He said he went through a list of 'most popular wedding sites' and Grace was first. The Palace of Fine Arts was second. He said it was 'bad luck' he got there too late to save her."

"Did he see who did it?"

Nick shrugged, but I practically felt the anger on him that time.

"He says no. He's promised to cooperate, says he'll give us whatever we want in terms of his own investigation. He also claimed he'd been operating on a hunch with the Palace thing or he would have brought us in earlier. He claims he never expected to hit paydirt...not that fast, anyway."

I nodded, folding my hands across my chest as I studied his eyes.

"But you still don't believe it?" I said cautiously.

"Fuck no, I don't believe it!" Nick exploded, staring at me. "Do you?"

I kept my expression clinician smooth. "Is there any reason why I shouldn't?"

He aimed a finger at me.

That time, the anger practically vibrated off his skin.

"You were *there*, Miri," he said. "You saw him in there. Did he look like someone scared to you? Of the police? Of me? Of any of us? Did he strike you as someone likely to 'cooperate to the full extent of the law'? Who even gave a shit the girl was dead, for that matter?"

I hesitated, then shrugged. "Is there any reason I should dismiss his explanation out of hand? Is there a more plausible story, given the facts?"

"You think him just *happening* to be there, trying to save that girl's life, is more plausible than him getting caught murdering her?"

Thinking about his words, I nodded, telling the truth.

"Frankly? Yes. If the girl's parents actually hired him, Nick—"

"The whole thing is b.s., Miri...and you know it is!"

Thinking about his words, I shook my head slowly. "Sorry, Nick. I don't. It's weird, sure...and his being at the scene definitely makes him a suspect. But as stories go, it's not entirely implausible either." I tapped Quentin Black's business card against the top of my desk. "Maybe you don't want to admit he might have followed a lead that you missed and it paid off?"

Nick's complexion darkened. "You *yourself* said Black's a fucking sociopath—"

"There are a lot of high-functioning narcissists and people with personality disorders running around who don't become serial killers, Nick," I reminded him mildly. "I imagine there are a fairly high number in various forms of law enforcement... as well as in private security. Studies have shown there are certainly a lot running around with big stock portfolios. Without a motive, I can't imagine why you wouldn't at least entertain his story as the true one." Clearing my throat, I added, "Anyway, I said I *thought* he was a sociopath...not that I knew for certain he was one. It's way too early for me to make a diagnosis like that definitively."

Pausing, I kept my voice casual.

"What else?"

"What do you mean, what else?"

"Did you find out anything more about Black? Something you're not telling me?"

"Like what?"

Shrugging lightly, I kept my voice nonchalant as I took another sip of coffee. "Well. His fingerprints and DNA didn't show up, even though he's a P.I....a licensed P.I., according to you. Did you find out why? Is he ex-intelligence or something? Someone with a high clearance, that they waived that for him?"

Nick stared at me, his dark eyes hard as stones. "Why the fuck would you ask me that?"

I sighed at the wariness in his gaze.

"Nick," I said, lowering the cup. "I'm about to marry someone in intelligence, remember? And Black pegged me as ex-military less than a minute after I walked through that door. It stands to reason that he might—"

"Okay, okay," Nick cut in, holding up a hand. He still sounded angry. "And yes. He did a few stints. And yes, Special Forces at the end. Which means it's all sealed...even to me." He gave me a more pointed look. "Ian might be able to access it, though."

I frowned, feeling somehow that the mention of Ian was a little too deliberate.

"He's out of town," I said, my frown deepening. "And I wouldn't count on it anyway, not unless you went through channels. Do you have anyone else you like for this? For the Grace Cathedral killing at least?"

"No," Nick said, his voice harder.

I sighed for real that time, setting my coffee back on the desk. "What is it with you and this guy, Nick? This isn't like you. Is it so hard to admit you might have been wrong?"

"It is when I know I'm not wrong."

I let out a snort, making an *I give up* gesture with my hands. Nick continued to glare at me though.

"There's something not right about this guy, Miri. I know you see it."

I let out a surprised laugh. "Well, yeah...read between the lines, Nick. He was probably doing wet-work for the U.S. military...for all we know he still is. Of course you're getting vibes. Has it occurred to you that maybe you just don't like guys like him?"

When I met Nick's gaze, his eyes looked positively murderous.

"Do you *know* this guy, Miri?" he said.

"Know him?" I felt my face grow inexplicably hot. "Black?"

"Yes, Black. Do you know him? Had you met him before yesterday?"

I gaped at him. "Why in God's name would you think that?"

"It's a simple fucking question. Are you going to answer it?"

My jaw snapped shut. "No, I don't *know* him." My temper sparked hotter when I felt Nick not believing me. "Just what are you asking me, Nick? Or do I even want to know?"

He didn't answer at first. When he looked back at me though, his anger hadn't lessened. If anything, the expression in his eyes looked even colder.

"He's been asking about you, Miri. A lot."

I let out an annoyed sound, unimpressed. "And? How is that my fault?"

"He also asked me about Ian. Made a few cryptic fucking remarks I didn't like much, truthfully. Things that made me wonder if maybe he knew Ian, too."

I firmed my lips. Raising my hand, I tapped my engagement ring, a perversion of me and Nick's running joke. I let my hand fall back to the top of my desk.

"He made it clear he noticed the ring, Nick," I said.

"And?" Nick said. "You fit the victim profile, Miri. He knew Ian's name. He also knew Ian was a defense contractor. Are you sure all of this isn't about you?"

It was my turn to stare.

Not about Nick's revelations about what Black knew, at least not primarily. After all, I was pretty sure I knew exactly how Quentin Black obtained that information.

No, I stared more because it hadn't even occurred to me until then that I fit the wedding killer's profile. Ian and I weren't to be married for another five months, and I'd barely had time to even think about ceremony itself, so maybe that was part of it. With him gone so much lately, a lot of the planning had been put on hold. I didn't have a living mother to pester me about it, and Ian's parents were both dead too, so we'd opted for a pretty simple ceremony.

The fact that I fit the victim profile stunned me briefly.

It also made me wonder what Black was up to, grilling Nick about Ian.

Was he threatening me via Nick? I found it hard to believe, although I couldn't have said why exactly. If he wasn't threatening me, what the hell was he doing? Why antagonize a homicide cop who likes you for murder? Was Black really that arrogant?

Yes, my mind answered unequivocally. *Yes, he really is that arrogant.*

I wondered if there was more to it, though. Had he done it simply to rattle Nick, or had it been some kind of message to me? Or was it more to drive a wedge between me and Nick?

Thinking about the possibilities made my face heat again.

Still, if it was anger or something else I felt, I couldn't decide.

Realizing I'd been staring over Nick's shoulder while I'd been thinking those things rather than looking at Nick himself, I refocused on his face.

Once I did, I found him watching me, that harder, more suspicious scrutiny back in his eyes.

"What the fuck is going on, Miri?" he said. "You're not telling me something. I want to know what it is."

I rolled my eyes, annoyed for real that time. "You're imagining things, Nick—"

He cut me off.

"I'm really not. So I'm going to say this once, Miri. Stay the hell *away* from this asshole. That's a direct order."

"An order?" I said, disbelieving. "I'm not in your *platoon* anymore, Sarg..."

He didn't flinch. "Order. Threat. Warning. Pick a word. And don't think I don't see the wheels turning in that giant brain of yours, Miriam. Don't think for a single second that I didn't see it when I told you that asshole was going free today, too..."

Grunting, he rearranged his muscular body in the chair.

"Truthfully, I wasn't going to give you that damned card," he muttered, motioning towards my desk. "I was just going to kick you off the case, let you think we were proceeding with Black the same as we would with any other murdering asshole..." Taking a breath, he sank deeper into the leather, planting his hands on the armrests. "...Ian's going to kill me if I tell him about this, you know. That I let you talk to a fucking *serial killer* who now has a hard-on for you. An ex-spook who got his record expunged for being a professional murderer..."

Biting my lip at the reference to Ian, I only shrugged.

"So why did you give me the card, Nick?" I said.

He glared at me, then motioned sharply with a hand. "Because for awhile there, you were almost acting like *yourself* again, Miri..."

"As opposed to what?"

His expression dropped every ounce of sarcasm.

"As opposed to someone who's *lying* to me," he said. Staring at me coldly, he motioned to where I still held Quentin Black's business card between my fingers, toying with the paper without noticing I was doing it. "I don't know what it is, but you've got some kind of 'thing' with this guy. That, or he's managed to snow you in some way...intrigue you maybe. Maybe it's some shrink thing...a profile you've never seen before. Maybe you liked bantering with a brain even bigger than yours for once. I know that must be a rare experience for you..."

Glaring at me, he made his voice more threatening.

"Or maybe you fucking *know* him, Miri. Maybe you met him over in the sand pits, on R&R or something. Maybe you slept with him over there...dated him. Played chess with him. Cleaned his rifle. Whatever."

When I gaped at him, he held up a hand.

"Frankly, I don't care. That part's none of my damned business. What I *do* care about, is that you're not thinking clearly around him. And I'm not the only one who's noticed."

I continued to stare at him, as much in disbelief as anything.

I couldn't help wondering what Black had said to him.

71

Clearly, he'd said things about me, not just about Ian. Black was feeding this line to Nick that he knew me in some way. But why? What possible motive could he have? And what the hell had he said to rattle Nick like this? To have him looking at me like I was the damned enemy?

For the first time in a long time, I was really tempted to read Nick.

On purpose I mean...something I never did with friends.

I picked up things on accident sure, no matter how much I shielded. But actually *going* there, trying to get inside a friend's brain, that was a major no-no for me.

I shoved the fleeting temptation out of my mind the instant it rose.

"Nick," I said instead, my voice openly puzzled. "You were watching me the whole time I spoke to Black. You practically high-fived me when I came out of there—"

"And you've been acting weird ever since," he cut in.

"You were *there*, Nick," I said angrily. "You heard the whole interview!"

"I was there," he acknowledged, gripping the armrests of the leather chair. "And I did hear it. But I strongly suspect I didn't hear *all* of it, Miriam. Now why is that, do you think?"

I flinched before I could stop myself.

Then I bit my lip.

"Meaning what?" I said, my voice neutral.

"Meaning that!" he snapped, motioning at my mouth. "Meaning what you *just did,* right there! Meaning those weird silences between you two in the box...and the time you nearly fell out of your damned chair, just looking at him. I didn't think much of it at the time, but I noticed. Even before I talked to Black, Glen asked me why you two seemed to know each other..."

When I avoided his eyes, anger leaked out more aggressively in his voice.

"Are you going to tell me the truth?" he said. "Did you meet him over there? In some fucking sand cave outside Kabul?"

I shook my head, staring at him incredulously. "No."

"Do you know him at all? From before we picked him up?"

"No!" I said, angrier.

He continued to level that stare at me. I could feel the skepticism on him. More than skepticism. He flat out thought I was lying to him.

As if he heard me, Nick let out a forced sigh, clenching his jaw briefly. "I don't know what it is about the two of you, but everything in my cop instincts tells me to keep you as *far away* from that piece of shit ghost as possible. So that's what I'm going to do."

Exhaling in annoyance, I started to speak but Nick cut me off.

"I mean it, Miri," he said, holding up a hand.

He leaned forward, glaring at me.

"You go near that guy, I'll arrest you. You hear me? I don't give a damn what Ian says. I'll throw you in jail until we have enough to haul Black back in...and then I'll slap you with interfering with an open murder investigation. Make you go in front of a judge...even if they throw it out."

I stared at him, unable to hide my incredulity.

"Jesus, Nick. What in the hell —"

"I know you better than you think, Miri," Nick said, his voice colder still.

There was a silence where we just looked at one another.

As we did, it hit me that I'd never been on the receiving end of that particular look in Nick's eyes before.

I'd seen it, sure, but I'd never had it aimed at me.

He didn't just think I was holding out on him.

He *knew* I was holding out on him. He knew there was something about Quentin Black I wasn't telling him.

And he didn't like it.

He didn't like it one bit.

FIVE

ONE OF OURS

I'VE NEVER LIKED BEING TOLD WHAT TO DO.

It's a character flaw, I know.

But it is what it is.

Now that I knew they might be letting Black go later that day, my window felt suddenly short. I knew how the release system usually worked. I also knew Nick. He'd find some excuse to keep Black there as long as he possibly could...at least until mid-afternoon. Longer if he could get away with it. They'd run him through hoops until his lawyer threw a fit. Knowing Nick, Black would get out right around the end of the workday, somewhere around five or six o'clock.

Four or four-thirty at the earliest.

So I had some time, but not a lot.

Nick finally left my office around eight o'clock. Not long after that, I saw three clients, including the one I'd blown off the day before, pretty much one after the other.

Then it was noon.

After the last one finally left—and I pretty much had to shove him out the door, since he was one of those needy, clingy types—I spent a few minutes looking over the website of one

Black Security and Investigations Firm, sole proprietor, Mr. Quentin R. Black.

I didn't learn much.

Other than a basic list of services and some impressive names on his testimonials list, his website was frustratingly vague, if beautifully designed.

Chasing down his clients didn't yield much either.

I knew some of that had to be due to the nature of his work. Even so, I found myself wondering if he had people on his payroll who knew how to get a good chunk of his web presence blocked from regular search engines. I didn't come across a single picture of him online, not even on his own website. I briefly contemplated calling his firm's front desk, then decided I would rather go in person. I knew there was a good chance his office would have surveillance cameras but I was willing to risk that too.

Anyway, Black had been taunting me. Might as well return the favor.

Grabbing my keys off the hook near my office door, I only paused long enough to feed Gomey an excuse about a headache and how I'd decided to work the rest of the afternoon from home. As I battled the traffic to make my way downtown on California Street, I told myself that I needed to do this...that I had a kind of civic duty to check him out personally, given that most people would have no idea what they were dealing with in Black.

I told myself I just wanted to see his workspace.

Gather a few impressions.

I knew it would be easier to check him out in the psychic sense later on, if I got a good look at where he worked. There was some kind of weird relationship between knowing a person's physical location and being able to see them with my mind.

I knew that was only part of it though.

If I was being wholly honest with myself, I was planning on doing something I hadn't done in years, not since I'd gone looking for Zoe's killer and found nothing. I was planning on actively using my psychic ability to investigate something. Mostly, I was hoping I could get enough off Black's employees to form a more complete picture of Mr. Black himself. Maybe then I could decide if Nick was right about him.

I knew Nick very well *might* be right about him.

But I needed to know for myself.

I got something different off Black than what Nick did. I couldn't yet put it into words, but I was reasonably sure it wasn't only the psychic thing that Black and I shared. I knew it might be that, however. I knew Nick might be right about me, in thinking I just didn't want to believe Black could be a psychopathic killer, even if my reasons were different from what Nick thought.

I just had to hope Nick wouldn't return to my office in the next few hours.

I pulled into an underground parking structure three blocks from Black's office building about fifteen minutes later. Taking only my phone and my purse, I walked up to the faceted, cylindrical tower and felt my throat tighten as I saw the stepped fountain standing in a sidewalk garden in front of the building. The seven-story glass-enclosed lobby I could see behind the garden looked like something out of a movie.

Even for this part of town, the building was high-end.

I recognized it, although I'd never been inside.

That feeling of unreality worsened when I went through the revolving door and found myself standing in front of a waterfall fountain coming out of one wall and decorated with hanging crystals that shimmered with pale, colored lights. Real art hung on the walls. It was like they'd made a section of the lower lobby into an adjust of the San Francisco MOMA.

I hadn't made it halfway across the granite tile floor before I was approached by someone in a security uniform. I'd been looking down, noticing that the floor was designed like an elaborate chess board as I aimed my feet for the main bank of elevators, when the guard stepped right in front of me, forcing me to halt.

Smiling, he asked me politely which business I intended to visit.

When I told him, he excused himself to wander a few feet away and murmur something into his sleeve. I noticed he never really took his attention off me, however.

I wondered if he'd tackle me to the ground if I made a break for the elevators.

I strongly suspected he would.

He touched his ear after he stopped talking into his sleeve and only then did I notice he wore an earpiece as well. So this building didn't have rent-a-cops...it had its own Secret Service, including the requisite toys that intimidated as much as provided function.

Just when I'd started to think I was about to be booted out that revolving door for not having an appointment, the guard's expression cleared.

Nodding to something someone said on the other side of the line, he smiled.

Turning towards me, he winked, and widened that smile at me.

Huh, I thought.

He took his hand off his ear and motioned for me to follow him.

He looked genuinely friendly now as he escorted me off to the side and down a narrow corridor past the security desk and to the left of the main bank of elevators. I couldn't help wondering why I got the nod, and assumed it must be because I wore a suit, was female and happened to be wearing high heels that day.

Sometimes, being a well-dressed woman didn't suck.

Even so, I glanced back at that row of gleaming elevators as we left them behind, wondering why he wasn't taking me to them. I suddenly envisioned myself being strip-searched in a windowless room. Pulling my jacket tighter around my skirt suit and trying not to frown, I only relaxed after I read the guy briefly and realized he was just taking me to a different set of elevators.

A few seconds later we reached the alcove I'd seen in his head when I took a quick peek at his thoughts. Only one elevator sat in that alcove, and it looked strangely smaller and older than the ones I'd glimpsed from the main lobby.

It also looked considerably more fancy, with copper-colored plating on the outside doors rather than the brushed steel of the main bank. An art deco-styled arrow pointed at only five numbers set in the wall, all of which were also fashioned of copper.

So apparently this was the express elevator. It served only floors 44, 45, 46, 47 and 48.

The guard used a pass card to open the elevator doors.

Smiling at me again, he motioned politely for me to enter, then entered after me, making me nervous all over again. But he only used his pass card to activate the button for floor 48 before he exited, nodding to me in a friendly way as the doors closed between us.

I breathed a sigh of relief once I found myself alone.

Even so, I found myself looking up, scanning the inside of

79

the mirrored car with its brass railings until I found the God's eye camera. Frowning up at it, I looked down at the emerald green carpet on the floor of the elevator, then at the five numbered buttons.

The elevator moved fast.

I mean, it really booked.

It climbed those stories faster than I was prepared for... not really giving me time to think through what I intended to say when I reached Black's offices. I also had only a minute or two to think about the possible ramifications of Black definitely knowing I'd been here, and how I felt about that, as well.

But maybe he wouldn't know.

After all, they must get walk in clients occasionally. Would they really run every face and ID by Quentin Black himself, when he owned the company?

It struck me as unlikely.

The thought made me relax, if only a little.

When the doors opened with a melodic ping a few seconds later and I walked out, I found myself in another glass-enclosed lobby. Tall windows stood to either side of the elevator's foyer, and the ceiling directly overhead was all glass, too. Remembering we were essentially housed in the penthouse floor of the building, I forced myself to exhale after I'd looked up at a swath of blue sky and high, white cumulous clouds, taking in the view for a few seconds before I steeled myself and looked straight ahead.

A brushed copper door stood directly in front of me, a decidedly more modern version than the art deco style of the elevators. The door stood unusually wide and tall, with a long, vertical cylinder for a handle, about the width of a copper pipe.

Etched into the translucent, plate glass walls that angled back on either side of that door was the same eagle symbol that had been on Black's business cards. The glass formed a near pyramid shape with the copper door at one end and diagonal hallways on either side. I couldn't see through either of the long windows, or even see shapes moving inside, but the effect of all that glass made it look strangely like the prow of a ship.

This had to be the place.

Were they really the only business on this floor? Or were more offices located at the end of both of those dimly-lit, angled corridors?

Even as my mind posed the question, a door opened somewhere down the corridor to my left. I heard it rather than saw it, just as I heard footsteps coming towards me from that same hall, moving purposefully over the plush carpet.

They weren't loud, but the sound carried, probably due to acoustics.

I reached out with my mind, but got nothing.

Silence.

Nerves slid over me, intense enough that I considered retreat. I considered walking straight into the offices of Black Securities and Investigations...then I considered just leaving, getting back in the art deco elevator and returning to the ground floor.

Before I could make up my mind, the person walking towards me reached the natural light of the lobby through the high glass walls and windows.

Once he had, I could only stare.

It was Quentin Black himself.

Moreover, he was shirtless, wearing only black dress pants. I couldn't help staring at his bare chest and the rest of the way down his body to his bare feet before my eyes jerked back up to his face.

His hair was wet, like he'd just gotten out of the shower.

He had tattoos on his inner arms...tattoos I hadn't seen when he was covered in blood.

He didn't have much body hair, I noticed.

"Hello, doc," he said.

He raised a hand in a strangely dated-looking greeting.

Before I could manage to form words, he motioned with his head back down the corridor from which he'd come.

"Do you mind?" he said. "I'm not fully decent." His sculpted lips lifted in a faint smile. "I confess, I considered just summoning you the other way...but I thought you might not react entirely well to that. From the look on your face, I suspect I am right."

He continued to study me when I didn't answer, that faint scrutiny in his eyes.

Then, all at once, he was done.

"Come along then," he said. "It's just down here."

Without another word, he turned on his heel, moving lightly and with an unmistakable grace. I again got fighter as I followed him with my eyes.

That impression strengthened as he continued to walk. I watched him retreat back down that dimly-lit corridor until I couldn't see him anymore and it struck me that it probably wasn't another office that lived down there.

It was his actual residence.

After another, stuttered breath of a pause, I found myself following him.

JUST A MOMENT," HE SAID TO ME, AFTER HE'D MOTIONED ME INTO another high-ceilinged foyer. I found myself staring past him at a massive window on the other side of a sunken living room with plush, pale green carpet. My jaw was hanging, but he continued speaking in the same casual tone, as if I'd been there a dozen times before.

"I'd prefer if we were alone before we talked..." he added. "Give me a minute, will you?"

It took a few seconds for his words to penetrate.

Then I jerked my eyes off the view through that window, where I could see the Bay Bridge with Oakland in the background past Yerba Buena Island. I looked up at him, and a jolt went through me when I realized how tall he was.

"Alone?" I said. "Did you say alone?"

Those flecked gold eyes met mine. "Yes."

"You mean we're not alone now?"

He tilted his head sideways.

I guessed it was a shrug? Something about the gesture struck me as even more alien than his gold eyes.

Remembering that I'd sat across from this man in chains only about 36 hours ago, I found myself noticing yet again just *how* tall he was, how broad his shoulders and how those muscles in his arms and chest didn't look any smaller when he wasn't wearing a shirt.

I felt my breath tighten as he watched me look at him.

"Meaning what?" I said.

He stepped away from me. I noticed suddenly that he held my jacket in his hands. He must have removed it while I'd been gaping out his living room window.

He took another step away from me, but those gold eyes remained on my face.

"Meaning...yes. There is someone else here. Obviously. I'll take care of it."

"Take care of it?" I continued to stare at him, fighting to make sense of his words. For some reason, what he was saying still wasn't quite computing.

He shrugged more normally the second time, his expression still wholly unapologetic.

Even so, I got the strangest impression that I made him nervous in some way.

That might have been funny if I wasn't still trying to decide if I'd just followed a real-life serial killer into his home and let him take my coat.

Looking away from me after another strangely loaded pause, he turned towards the door of a closet set into the wall near the edge of the foyer. Rather than hanging my jacket up on a hanger or even a hook, he simply opened the door and tossed it inside, then shut the door with a click.

I watched him do it, fighting a sudden, absurd desire to laugh.

A female voice rose from the back room. "Hey, sexy man! Where did you go?"

I froze.

Suddenly, I understood. Like really understood.

He had company. Not business-type company. The other kind.

My skin flushed.

Before I could think of what to say, he raised his voice.

"Hey!" he said. Hesitating, he seemed to be thinking. "... You." He frowned, still thinking. "...Person. I need you to leave... something's come up."

I stared at him incredulously, fighting another insane desire to laugh. "You don't know her name? And you're really *shouting* at her to leave? From here?"

He gave me a questioning look.

Then, without a word, he walked away from me, moving silently on shoeless feet. Again, I couldn't help but note that odd grace of his, somewhere between a martial artist and a dancer. He glanced back at me long enough to motion towards the couch.

"Sit," he said.

It sounded closer to a command than an offer.

Staring at his heavily-muscled back and the large, stylized dragon tattoo that crawled over most of it, I folded my arms as he walked away from me and into another part of his apartment. I didn't move from the foyer after he'd left, staring around his living room as I tried to decide what to do.

I still hadn't regained my balance from any of this. Part of me thought I should open the door and leave before he came back.

Assuming he let me go, that is, and didn't lock me out of the elevator.

Either way, I was way past quietly checking out his background at this point, under the radar of both him and Nick. I was in his damned home.

Nick might really arrest me for this.

I was still standing roughly where Black had left me when he walked briskly back into the main room.

This time, he wasn't alone.

One of his tanned hands clamped around the upper arm of a woman who was trying to both keep up with him and shove her foot into a four-inch heeled pump at the same time. She was muttering at him angrily as she walked. Her shirt was still halfway unbuttoned as he steered her, and untucked from the

85

black pencil-skirt she wore under a white silk dress shirt and black suit jacket.

"I still don't get what business would come up now, while we were—"

She glanced up to see me and came to a dead stop.

"What the fuck?" she burst out.

I couldn't help noticing that her lipstick was smeared, her blond hair tousled.

"What the fuck is this?" she demanded, waving the high-heeled shoe at me. "Is this your so-called 'business emergency'? You stopped in the middle of giving me head because a better offer came along?"

I winced.

Black didn't. Instead he gave me a puzzled look, as if thinking about her question. Then he looked back at her. He looked about to answer, but she turned, hitting him squarely in the chest with the sharp end of her shoe.

"You complete *dick*. Is this your fucking wife? Are you *married*?"

"No," he said absently. He resumed steering her towards the door and, blanching, I found myself moving into the living room if only to get out of their way.

She didn't seem to be listening to him though. She glared at me with some of the bluest eyes I'd ever seen as they walked past me. "Your husband's a prick. You know that? A total fucking prick..."

I could only gape at the two of them.

"He gives good head though," she sneered, still obviously trying to make me angry. Glaring up at him next, she added, "... At least when he bothers to finish."

He might not have even heard her, from his tone.

86

"Feel free to use the card I gave you," he said, his voice polite as he continued to steer her towards the door of his apartment. "I can't promise I'll be available..."

She let out another incredulous snort, swinging at him again with the shoe.

She glared at me from the door, even as he reached for the handle. He opened it in one smooth move. She swung the heeled shoe at his head that time but he ducked it easily, his expression still neutral as he moved behind her. With an insistent but not really a *rough* push, one hand on the small of her back and the other still gripping her arm, he guided her without preamble through the opening of the door.

Then he released her, leaving her in the corridor.

Before she could turn around, he closed the door firmly behind her.

From the outside, she banged on the door with her shoe, raising her voice.

"Asshole!" I heard muffled through the wood. "Fucking asshole!"

I think my mouth was still hanging open when my eyes shifted from the door back up to his face. He now wore a shirt at least, although it still hung open over his chest. I watched as he began to button it up. Watching him dress himself, hearing the woman curse at him from outside the door, I fought another absurd desire to laugh.

"You didn't sit down," he said, frowning slightly as he worked the catches of his shirt.

I shut my mouth with a snap, folding my arms.

The woman continued to curse at him from the hallway.

"One moment," he said, turning from me.

I watched as he walked to a low table in the living room,

scooping up what looked like a hands-free phone from the glass surface.

He fitted it around his ear. Touching a button on one side he spoke at once.

"I have a situation here," he said. "In the hallway outside my residence. Can you handle it? I have a meeting. And don't interrupt me for the rest of the afternoon."

He didn't appear to wait for an answer but clicked the same button on the hands-free and unhooked the earpiece from his ear, tossing it on the same glass table. He looked up at me, buttoning his sleeve cuffs now that the front of his shirt was done up.

"Would you like a drink?" he said.

Again, I got the oddest feeling from him that I made him nervous.

It was such a different reaction from how he spoke to me in that interrogation room, much less how he'd talked to the blond just now, I frowned, more confused than anything.

Making up my mind in the same set of seconds, I followed him the rest of the way into the living room. Without preamble, I walked directly to a white leather chair and sat, folding one leg precisely over the other.

"A drink?" he repeated.

"Something non-alcoholic, sure."

He nodded, once.

Even the nod looked strange on him.

When he retreated into the kitchen, which was open with long lights hanging down from the ceiling over a granite-topped bar, I turned my head, looking over my shoulder to speak to him.

"Are you going to tell me what the hell that was all about?" I said mildly.

He'd just finished gargling water and spitting it out in the sink. I looked away, grimacing when I remembered the woman's words. When I looked up next, he met my gaze from behind the open, stainless-steel refrigerator door. His voice conveyed genuine surprise.

"You need an explanation for that?"

Thinking about his words, I felt my frown deepen.

"No," I sighed. "I guess not." I looked back at him, watching him pour me a glass of what looked like rose-tinted water. "What am I doing here, Mr. Black? You must know I had no intention of visiting you here..."

"Planning a little B&E, were we?" he said, giving me a faint smile from behind the bar. "I find I am doing that very same thing. Great minds think alike..."

Breaking and entering. Cute.

"Hardly," I retorted. "I didn't even know you lived in the building."

He nodded absently, but didn't seem interested in pursuing that line of discussion.

Capping the glass jug with the rose-tinted water, he stuck the container back in the door of his fridge then walked the two glasses around the bar and back towards me. Handing me one as he passed, he sank into the couch across from me, laying an arm on the back cushion and staring at me levelly. Like in the interrogation room, he didn't hide his appraisal at all.

"You're a P.I.," I said finally.

"Obviously," he said. "Why would we discuss what you already know?"

Thinking about that, I pursed my lips. "Okay." Thinking again, I looked up. "Did you kill that girl?"

"You must know what I told your handsome cop about that?"

"I know what you *told* him, yes."

There was a silence.

Then he sighed, letting out a strange sound, a kind of clicking of his tongue on the roof of his mouth. Leaning forward, he rested his forearms on his thighs, measuring me again with his eyes.

"How did you get here?" he said.

I frowned, staring at him. Taking a sip of the rose-colored water, I was surprised to find it was some kind of fruit juice, and extremely fresh.

"Pomegranate," he said absently. "Are you going to tell me? How you got here?"

"I drove," I said, giving him a perplexed look. "I took the elevator. Who cares?"

He made that clicking sound again. That time, he sounded openly impatient.

"Here," he said. "How did you get *here?*" He motioned around us, including the view out the windows on all sides of us.

"San Francisco?" I said, still confused. "I was born here. Why? Where are you from? I can hear the accent...but I admit, I can't place it at all."

His frown deepened.

Before I could pursue that line of questioning, or make sense of the stare he continued to level at me, he regained his feet. I watched him walk to the long window facing the bay. He folded his arms, gazing out over the view without seeming to see it. When he turned to stare at me, his mouth was set in a harder frown.

"Can I have some of your blood?"

I froze. "What?"

Seeing my expression, he made that clicking sound again. "Not like that. I simply want a sample. With a syringe. Hygienically."

"What the hell for?"

Before he could answer, I found myself standing as well, placing the glass of juice on his glass table with more deliberation than necessary. I saw him watch me do it, even as he turned to face me, his feet planted evenly as he refolded his arms.

"Look," I said, waving off my own question. "Forget it. I don't think I want to know. In fact, I think I'd better go."

Turning, I started to make my way to his front door.

Before I could reach for the handle of his closet, the same closet where he'd tossed my jacket when I first came inside, he stood between me and it. I froze again, staring up at him as he put his muscular bulk between me and the exit to his apartment.

"Get out of my way," I told him, my voice a low warning.

"Does that cop know you are here?" he said, narrowing his gaze down at me. "Your friend. He doesn't know, does he?"

I felt myself tense even more. Was that a threat?

He glanced down at my arms and legs, as if sensing I was gearing up for the possibility that I might have to fight him. He exhaled in a kind of sigh, and that time, the expression on his face bordered on frustrated.

Or maybe that was still impatience I saw in his gold eyes.

"Don't you want to know what I was really doing there?" he said, his sculpted lips still tilted in a slight frown. "At the park yesterday morning?"

"Sure," I said, folding my own arms. "What were you really doing there, Mr. Black?"

"I was hunting," he said at once.

"Hunting?" I said, feeling my jaw tense again.

91

"Yes."

"Girls? Or serial killers?"

"Neither," he said. Then he shrugged, as if rethinking his words. "...Or perhaps both. I was hunting one of ours."

Refocusing on me, he frowned again, probably from the perplexed look I aimed at him.

He looked me over in a single flick of his gold eyes.

"Not human," he clarified. When I still didn't speak, he repeated with more emphasis, "...One of *ours*. Of course, I now think it's possible they might be killing these humans for sport. I'm just not sure why. I'd hoped you'd help me find out."

I stared up at him.

That time, I had no idea what to say to him at all.

SIX
QUESTIONS

W HAT DID YOU MEAN BEFORE?" I WATCHED HIM FROM WHERE
I stood in the middle of his sunken living room, my
voice openly wary. "One of ours? One of our *whats*,
if you don't mind my asking?"

He acted like he hadn't heard me.

For the last minute or so, I'd been watching him pace and
think.

He didn't seem to be over the fact that I'd insisted I was
human.

Yes, as in my insisting to him that I was actually a human
being.

Now he leaned over his kitchen bar, staring down at an
electronic tablet resting on the black counter. Now that I stood
next to it, I realized the bar wasn't granite at all but some denser,
more-expensive looking stone. It almost looked volcanic.

Black might have been working from the concentrated look
in his eyes, or perhaps he was just actively ignoring me.

I was about to give up, to just walk out for real, when he
spoke.

"Would you like to accompany me?" he said, tapping

through a sequence on the tablet without looking up. "I was more or less serious about the B&E. I plan to go tonight."

That strange nervousness I'd seen on him when I'd first gotten to his apartment seemed to have vanished. He was back to treating me with almost a clinical detachment.

"Go where?" I said, bewildered. "What do you mean, B&E?"

"I wasn't lying to your Inspector Tanaka about going through a list of the most frequently-used wedding sites," he said, not looking up from whatever he was doing on the tablet.

"...But I misspoke. I should have said wedding-*related* sites, not wedding sites per se. Which includes a number of locations beyond just those where actual marriage ceremonies frequently occur." He narrowed his eyes, sliding his finger across the front of the tablet. "So places where engagement photos are taken. Places where receptions occur...etc." Glancing up at me with those gold eyes, he added, "I can see why that might have been confusing."

"Where are you going tonight?" I asked again.

"I've created a sort of algorithm," he explained, again as if I hadn't spoken. "Probability factors for wedding-related activities to occur, combined with a subset for the other variables the killer has displayed..." He glanced up a second time, cocking an eyebrow at me. "I thought perhaps we could visit the next one on the list together."

"Which is where?" I said.

Again, he acted like he hadn't heard me.

I fought the interest out of my voice in spite of myself, trying to make it annoyance.

"Are you going to tell me where you're going or not?" I thought a few seconds more and added, "You know Nick'll have a tail on you?"

He met my gaze directly that time. His lips slid upwards in a faint smile. "By 'Nick,' I presume you mean Inspector Tanaka?"

I flushed, although I couldn't for the life of me have said why. "Yes."

"I am not concerned." He paused, studying my eyes. "Are you? I am guessing he told you to stay away from me. From what I saw, he very clearly *intended* to tell you to stay away from me when he left me in that interrogation room this morning. He seemed quite intent on bullying you on that point, if necessary..."

He smiled at me.

"I'm glad to see that he succeeded in that about as well as I expected."

I frowned.

Putting down my now-empty glass of pomegranate juice on his kitchen counter, it struck me again to wonder what I was doing. Rather than conducting any kind of examination, I think it was safe to say that I was now simply "hanging out" with Quentin Black at his apartment.

He seemed to be perfectly comfortable with that fact as well.

Moreover, now we were discussing a murder case we had no earthly business discussing.

No wonder Nick thought I had some kind of past with this guy.

"Did you read his mind for that?" I said, deciding to be direct.

"Yes," he said absently.

I watched him use his finger to slide open a new screen on the tablet. I wasn't close enough to see what he was looking at, so I sighed in frustration, and partly in defeat.

"What are you looking at?" I demanded.

"Specs for the building."

"*Which* building?" I said. "Are you really not going to tell me?"

"The Legion of Honor," he said, glancing up. "It's next on our list. I thought it best to break in tonight, when it is closed. I strongly suspect our friend will wait until it's closed as well...so we should endeavor to get there before he does."

"It's definitely a man then?" I said, catching his pronoun use.

He shrugged. "Statistical probability."

I fought not to ask him one of the dozen or so questions that rose to my mind. Exhaling in frustration when he didn't go on, I picked one and asked it anyway.

"What in God's name makes you think he'll be there tonight?" I said.

Exhaling some frustration of his own, he pointed vaguely at the sun through the plate glass window, which was already starting to sink in the sky.

"There are astrological reasons." He looked back at his tablet, now using both hands to manipulate the size of something on his screen. "Related to rituals," he added, turning his head as if looking at something on the screen from a different angle. "It's not so simple to explain. I told you the algorithm was somewhat complex...and that it involved several variables, including astrological ones..."

"No, you didn't."

"Well...I meant to," he said without a pause. "This particular system of astrology has to do with rituals, as I said. If our target is following the pattern I *think* he is following, we can expect three separate incidents related to this particular stage of the ritual.... and the third should be tonight. Unless, of course, we stop him."

I stared at Black's downturned head, frowning.

Sighing again, he raised his upper body, leaning his palms on the bar counter and looking at me directly.

"It is difficult to explain," he repeated. "It has to do with wedding rituals from our home world. Wedding rituals of *our* people," he added, in case I missed that part. "Clearly, our killer has weddings on the mind. He seems to have mixed feelings about them...wouldn't you agree?"

I folded my arms tighter, biting my lip.

"You're saying you're from another planet, Mr. Black?" I said tersely.

"Dimension," he said, leaning back over the tablet and using his fingers to slide the screen again. "Earth...but not this one. I'd really rather not talk about all that until I can get a look at your blood, if you don't mind." His voice grew preoccupied once more as he frowned at the screen. "Why don't we table that whole aspect of our discussion, doc? Now that I know you didn't 'immigrate' here knowingly, so to speak, I'd rather have something more concrete to show you before I explain things that are going to significantly alter your relationship to just about every aspect of your life...as well as your feelings of kinship towards the vast majority of this world's inhabitants."

My mouth opened. Since I couldn't think of anything to say to that however, I closed it a few seconds later with a snap.

"There are a number of clues your Inspector Tanaka has missed," Black added, without lifting his eyes from the screen. "Not his fault, really. I only noticed because I knew what I hunted. He would have no reason to look where I was looking."

"Meaning?" I said, my voice terse once more.

He looked up, exhaling in open impatience as he stared at me.

"This is all going to be much more difficult and time

consuming, if I have to walk you through even the *basics* of what I am doing every five seconds to keep you from having some kind of negative emotional reaction," he said. "I confess, I still want you with me. I would prefer if we could approach this in partnership. But it's going to be really tedious if I have to explain *every single reference* that comes up relating to our race. Can we please just table such things until we have the luxury to discuss them at our leisure?"

Closing the leather cover over the tablet with a magnetized-sounding snap, he stared at me, as if waiting for an answer.

"Y-yes?" I said, fighting with whether to be angry or not.

Or maybe whether it was worth arguing the point.

"Good." Exhaling in relief that time, he looked away, gazing out the window at the slowly dipping sun as if summoning every last ounce of his patience.

He faced me once he had.

"There are others here...of our kind," he explained in a short voice. "That's all you really need to know for now. I have no idea how many, so don't even ask. At least three. Likely not more than a few dozen, and frankly, that is pure optimism on my part. You are the first female I have encountered..." He hesitated, his stare flickering down my body. He seemed to shake something off before adding, "I have reason to believe that at least one of our kind here is ideological in an anti-human sense. He is also, I suspect, well-funded...and not particularly fond of me. But he is not located here."

"On this...world?"

"In this country," he corrected. Frowning at me, he said, "Why in the gods would I bring him up if he was still in our home dimension?"

Not sure what dimension he was talking about at that point,

for either of us, I started to ask, then decided to drop it. After all, he'd asked twice.

"Russia," he said, frowning back at me. "He's in Russia. In this dimension."

At my blank stare, he sighed again.

"Truly," he said. "That is not important now. I only bring it up in case it becomes relevant in relation to the rogue I've been tracking...the one who might be killing these human females and combining rituals from that other dimension and this one."

Staring off into the distance, a more thoughtful look on his face, he added, "I admit I am curious if these deaths are the work of one of ours who has simply gone insane...or if it is part of some more deliberate orchestration. Something with an end-goal that has wider implications."

"For who?"

He pretended not to hear my question.

He glanced over my body with another of those appraising stares. "I admit, the coincidence of finding you here, at the same time, strikes me as overly..." He paused, as if searching for the right word.

"...Coincidental," he finished.

For a long-feeling number of seconds we just looked at one another.

"The Velaquez family didn't really hire you, did they?" I said.

He gave me a disparaging look. "They could not even afford my consultation fee."

"How did you get them to say they had hired you?"

He gave me another look that translated more or less as *really?*

I bit my tongue, then pressed on. "So you've simply been

looking for this...*rogue*...on your own? And you think he might be the murderer?"

"Yes."

"*Why* are you looking for him, if no one is paying you?"

He frowned again, staring at me. "He is one of ours."

The silence deepened.

"Would you like to accompany me, Ms. Fox?" he asked.

That time, his voice sounded formally polite.

He really wanted me to go, I realized.

"How are you going to get there without Nick following you?" I said.

"By leaving now," he said, checking that expensive-looking military-style watch. "Well. Perhaps ten minutes from now. Soon."

"Now?" I said, startled. "I thought you said —"

He sighed in open impatience.

"I would prefer to conduct surveillance beforehand," he explained. "I can't find enough recent pictures of the exhibit layouts to get a sense of where he might stage this. I need to walk the grounds. I thought we could do that while they are still open...during business hours, I mean. It is not practical to remain inside for the duration, given what my staff tells me regarding the most efficient means of circumventing their security protocols. But we could go, look around, then eat dinner while waiting for my team to finish prep."

Glancing at my hand, the one wearing the engagement ring, he paused before making a strangely fluid gesture towards the ring itself. "It may have to be a long dinner," he said.

I shrugged. "Ian's out of town. Your timing is good, on that front at least. Although he's out of town most of the time these days..."

Trailing, I realized I was already talking as if I was going with him.

For a long moment, he only looked at me.

Then his eyes dropped back to the ring I wore.

"There are other things we could do, of course," he said somewhat cagily. "To pass the time."

I gave him a warier look. "Meaning?"

"I suppose sex is out of the question?" he said.

He cleared his throat, going on in an almost carefully polite voice. "While we wait. Clearly, you're in a relationship. But I don't know what kind of agreement you and this...Ian...operate under."

I let out a bewildered snort. "What?"

"I mean no offense." He met my gaze with those riveting gold eyes, his face still polite but essentially unapologetic. "It's a more pleasant way to pass the time than most. And I wanted to... clarify things. I admit I'm reacting to being around a female of my own kind more than I'd accounted for. Likely more than you realize. But you needn't worry on your own behalf," he added more sharply, maybe at something in my face. "...I am more than capable of controlling myself, Miriam."

Flinching at his use of my first name, I continued to stare, fighting somewhere between asking him what the hell he was talking about, reminding him what I'd walked in on that afternoon, making some mention of him being an active suspect in an ongoing investigation of *multiple homicides*...and giving a flat, unequivocal no on the sex part before I did any of that and confused the issue more.

I ended up falling roughly on the last of these.

"No," I said, incredulity leaking into my voice. "Absolutely no. Most definitely *not* on the agenda, Mr. Black. And yes, I'm in a relationship. I'm engaged. And no...that's definitely not okay with me or Ian. Absolutely not. No."

He nodded, seemingly unfazed.

Then he just stood there, his expression calm. It occurred to me after a few seconds more that he was still waiting for my definitive answer.

Not about sex.

About the other thing.

"And yes," I blurted. "I'll go. To the gallery, I mean. And to dinner at least, depending on what we find. But no....funny business, Mr. Black. Dinner. That's it."

He gave me another of those curt nods.

"Understood," he said. "Yes on the gallery and to dinner... with a pending 'maybe' on any subsequent B&E. Absolute no on any funny business between us. I agree to your terms."

From anyone else, it would have sounded like he was making fun of me.

From Black, it sounded more like an awkward attempt at reassurance. Perhaps even some kind of informal contract. When he said it, he even held up a hand in a strange sort of peace gesture. Or maybe it was more of a promise gesture—like a boy scout's salute, but less formal and he used all of his fingers.

As soon as it got quiet again between us, I wondered what the hell I was doing.

I'd given him a yes before I even let the rational part of my brain weigh in.

Nick would kill me. Arrest me, anyway.

He might even have grounds at this point, although I couldn't for the life of me think what those charges would be, since I was no longer officially on the case and Black had invited me into his home completely of his own volition.

Of course, if I accompanied Black into the Legion of Honor that night, Nick would *definitely* have grounds to arrest me. And how on earth would I explain that? I could just picture telling Nick I'd broken into a museum in the dead of night with a murder suspect to see if a serial killer from another dimension might show up.

The thought made me smile...if involuntarily. Then again, maybe I was giving the dark humor part of my brain a little too much free reign right now.

I knew some part of me was hooked, though.

I could admit that much to myself.

Remembering that Nick might know exactly where I was already, my humor faded still more. He might be waiting for me or Black to leave the apartment even now. After all, when I came here, it was with the understanding that Black remained in police custody.

Nick would have someone tailing Black. I was sure of it.

"Hey," I said, glancing at Black. "When they let you out. Did you happen to notice—"

"They definitely tailed me here, yes."

Black turned towards me from where he'd been putting the headset from the glass table into the pocket of a long coat I hadn't seen him put on.

He wore boots now too, I noticed.

I frowned at his words. "I thought you said you couldn't read me."

"I can't in the usual way. But I still catch things, here and there. And you aren't trying to hide yourself from me as much as you had been before, in that police station."

He said it matter-of-factly.

I thought about that, then shoved the possible implications

of those thoughts from my mind. I tried to decide where his accent originated instead. Sometimes it sounded almost Asian. He didn't look Asian, but he could be some obscure mix.

"He didn't come himself," Black added, shoving a smartphone with a wide screen into a different coat pocket. "...Tanaka," he clarified. "He might be out there *now*, of course, but he had someone else follow me from the station, likely in the hopes I wouldn't recognize the tail. There is still a good chance he doesn't know you are here, Miriam. Whoever he sent would likely not have been looking for you."

Before I could decide how to respond, he turned, heading for the corridor to the right of his foyer. I assumed his bedroom lived down there, given that he'd disappeared and reappeared from the same direction when he'd gone to fetch the blond.

The memory brought a faint smile to my face.

Then a more noticeable heat.

"I'll be right back," he informed me, glancing over his shoulder. "Just grabbing a few supplies." Without slowing his steps, he spoke over his shoulder again. "...And don't worry. We can get out via the roof. Your homicide detective won't see us, even if he is down there."

"The roof?" I muttered.

But Black had already gone.

I glanced upwards, as if I would be able to see what he was talking about through the wood-beamed high ceiling. Did he really have a helipad up there? It was the only thing that made sense. But was he seriously saying he was going to *helicopter* us out of there, just so we could commit crime undetected by the SFPD?

That didn't strike me as particularly inconspicuous.

Then again, as they always say...the rich really are different.

H E DID TAKE ME OUT VIA HELICOPTER.

He flew the damned thing, too.

It was only me and him, and for the first time that day, I found myself wanting to ask him about his security company, as well as about his military background.

Five black-uniformed security personnel waited for us on the roof when we took the stairs up there after spending some time in the immaculate offices of Black Securities and Investigations.

On the other side of that copper-coated door, I'd discovered that the offices really did form a kind of island on the segment of floor not taken up by Black's residence. As a result, unlike his apartment, it had no windows. None that I saw, anyway... which I supposed wasn't a terrible thing for a security company, although pretty redundant considering how hard it was to even get up here. Smokey glass walls partitioned much of the offices off inside the business suite, too, so a fair bit of privacy existed even between Black's agents.

I saw a lot of computers, of course, as well as a number of people doing what looked like research. I saw a lot of people on hands-free phones, too.

I only saw maybe twelve employees total on the main floor, but I suspected a lot more people worked for him who might be elsewhere. I glimpsed a few windowless offices in the back as well as a number of storage lockers that some part of me wondered about.

It was not a small-feeling operation.

It didn't feel huge either, but it definitely felt bigger than the name implied. Big enough that I wondered why I'd never heard of it before today.

All of his employees were polite. Deferential even.

Not just to Black...to me, too.

I got a few curious stares as we walked by, with a number of women and men double-taking me as I walked past. Black took me into a back room before we went up to the roof, and I soon realized in surprise that he'd done it so I could grab a change of clothes. Of course, when I thought about that, it made perfect sense. I didn't really want to be wearing a suit and heels during our break-in that evening, no matter how good of camouflage it might be beforehand.

He had clothes in a lot of different sizes...women's and men's.

It made me curious about his business all over again, but I didn't ask.

He instructed me on a few articles of clothing, including an armored vest, boots...and a shoulder holster for a gun. When I protested I didn't have a concealed carry license in California, nor could I legally use any of his guns, I expected him to tell me it wouldn't matter given what we planned on doing that night.

Instead, he said he'd already taken care of that.

I had absolutely no idea what that meant.

He gave me a faint smile. "This is the point that concerns you?" he said. "Illegal possession and carry of a firearm during our planned breaking and entering?"

I folded my arms. "I can potentially explain the latter."

"Can you?"

"Just... stop dodging the question," I said, waving a hand at him.

"I've made you my employee," he said, handing a dark dress

shirt to me over the partition I'd been using to try on clothes. Seeming to feel my reaction to his words, he added, "On a temporary and purely consultative basis, of course. At least until we can hammer out the details on something more permanent."

Looking over the partition, I gaped at him—again for maybe the twentieth or thirtieth time that day—then shook my head, pulling the shirt he'd handed me around my shoulders and buttoning it up. Only when I'd finished and was in the process of sliding an arm into the shoulder holster did I peer over the dark gray partition a second time, lifting an eyebrow.

"Fuck," he said, smiling faintly. "Stop flirting with me, doc. You're distracting me horribly."

I flinched, pulling my head back behind the partition, and I swore I heard him smile again. When I looked around the partition at him next, my face carefully blank, I saw zero apology in his eyes.

"We don't have a forensic psychologist," he explained. "It's a legitimate business expense. I've decided I need one on permanent staff."

"You put me on the payroll without asking me?"

Thinking briefly, he nodded. "No. Well... yes. Temporarily. Until we can negotiate something formal. Like I said." He quirked an eyebrow of his own. "Would you like to hear numbers?"

"No," I said, sure somehow they would be obscene. "Why?"

"I just told you why—"

"You know what I mean."

He gave me another flat look, holding his palms out without answering.

Clearly he thought his reasons were obvious.

Or irrelevant, maybe.

Exhaling in irritation, I said, "There's no possible way you got me a concealed carry permit in San Francisco in under two hours, simply because I'm on your staff as a contracted forensic psychologist." The disbelief remained overt in my voice. "Trust me, I know."

"I didn't do it through San Francisco. Or California at all."

I stared at him. "Meaning?"

He smirked, handing me a gun, handle first. "Stop stalling, doc. If the clothes fit, hand them over and put your street clothes back on. Or I'm going to get distracted again."

"You're really not going to tell me?" I said, shedding the holster and the shirt all over again and pulling back on my dress blouse. I glanced up to make sure he wasn't watching me, in spite of myself. "About the gun?"

He sighed as if bored. "You now have a special weapons permit, doc, through the DOJ. It allows for concealed carry when you are working under the auspices of Black Securities and Investigations." Giving my disbelieving look another faint smile, he glanced down, watching me button my top. Briefly, his eyes showed a flicker of heat.

"What about wait periods?" I said, maybe to distract him. "Background checks?"

"Waived the wait period," he said, glancing up. "And the written test. Oh... and the range test. They told me to try and get you to do all of those things, of course. We can talk about the details when we work on that thing where you join my staff permanently."

Ignoring that part, I shook my head.

"That's not possible," I told him flatly. "Not even for you."

He gave me another smile. Those gold eyes didn't waver.

"Who are you?" I said, unwilling to drop it. "Why would they do that for you?"

"They like me."

I couldn't help it. I let out an involuntary bark of a laugh.

Even so, like I'd been doing all day, in the end I let it go.

I handed back the holster too, watching him stuff it along with a gun in a canvas bag along with the clothes and boots he'd already picked out for me. I watched everything disappear when he zipped up the bag, but not before I noted that the gun he'd chosen for me was the new version of the 1911 MC Operator and a gun Nick would have drooled over.

When Black shoved a good half-dozen magazines into another bag, I simply watched.

He tossed two bullet-proof vests into that bag, as well.

Really, I told myself, he was right—a concealed carry permit wouldn't matter an iota, given what he intended me to do with the gun later that night. Even Black hadn't tried to convince me he had permission to break into the Legion after hours.

Still, some part of me found it ironic that he could hand out off-the-books gun permits like he was some kind of mafioso drug lord in a third world country, but he still had to commit petty crimes to hunt his so-called "rogue-dimensional-traveler."

The way his staff treated him didn't lessen my curiosity.

They all but genuflected when he walked by, and I noted not a single one of them joked with him or acted like they knew him personally at all.

They also asked absolutely no questions about who I was... or what we were doing... or even where we were going in the helicopter. In fact, I don't think I saw a single one of them ask Black *anything* that wasn't strictly relevant to what he needed in that precise moment. I definitely got a military vibe from many of them, too. A few tattoos I glimpsed on bare arms around the edges of form-fitting black T-shirts supported that impression.

Black didn't introduce me to any of them, or tell any of them my name.

The helicopter itself, which looked like some kind of modified military model rather than a rich guy's recreational toy, was a gunmetal gray with Black's eagle symbol on the doors.

He took the proffered headset handed to him by one of his staff and climbed into the cockpit as the man climbed out, presumably after conducting the initial pre-flight check. Black immediately started his own check once the guy vacated the cockpit, pausing only to motion me to take the seat across from him.

Watching another in his staff toss the three black bags into the cargo area of the helicopter, I approached cautiously, holding my hair and ducking down as I walked to where a very buffed-looking Asian woman wearing all black held the passenger door open for me.

Once I'd strapped in and clamped on my own headset, we were off.

The flight was short, but exhilarating, I admit.

What felt like bare minutes later, we landed on a helipad at the VA Hospital just south of Land's End Park, not far from the Sutro Baths and of course the Legion of Honor museum itself, which was in the northwestern corner of the adjacent Lincoln Park.

Black apparently either knew someone or made arrangements at the hospital itself, because one of his black-clad employees met us on the roof when we landed.

I watched that same employee hand Black what looked like a computerized car key before jerking open the back door of the helicopter and tossing our three bags of equipment out onto the helipad.

Then, exchanging places with Black in the cockpit seat, the man put on the pilot's headset.

Black hadn't powered all the way down when we landed, and now I watched, half-incredulous, as the employee powered it back up again. I stood there, holding my hair to keep it from whipping my face as I watched him take off. The aircraft rose in a nearly straight line, then its nose tilted down right before it headed back in the direction of downtown San Francisco. It was nearly out of sight before we'd even made it off the rooftop and inside the hospital's main building.

Despite our quick drop off and dust off, I was pretty sure it wasn't "normal" to use a government hospital helipad as your personal parking space...no matter how rich you were.

Even so, Black must have been training me already, because I didn't ask.

We carried the bags down to the parking lot and found the vehicle Black's employee left us by clicking the electronic car key a few times until something beeped. After we dumped the three bags into the trunk, we were on foot. We were also more or less in street clothes, although I wore a long coat Black had given me, and he still wore all black.

We walked to the Legion of Honor through the military base where the VA hospital lived, using back roads in Fort Miley to cut over to a footpath which brought us to the back end of the Legion and into Lincoln Park.

Once we entered the museum, Black got quiet, and unnervingly focused.

Mostly, I felt like I was watching him...and following him, without having much idea of what he was looking for precisely.

We did two quick circuits of the exhibit halls without stopping much at all.

Black had his large-screened phone out for most of that, and seemed to be looking at that as much as at any part of the physical layout. Any time a guard watched him for too long, Black started taking pictures, I noticed, but I couldn't tell if that was just a cover.

We lingered the longest in the courtyard.

Black also made a few circuits of the round exhibit room directly under the courtyard, the one below the glass pyramid that lived right by the main entrance to the building. Dominating that circle of light created by the pyramid was a bronze sculpture I didn't recognize.

I found myself looking at that sculpture far longer than anything else we saw.

It stood on a pedestal of blood-red marble, and depicted an angel on a winged horse, both with wings outspread. The angel held a scepter with a blood red jewel in the apex, but the jewel wasn't what caused me to stare.

It was the headpiece to the scepter itself, which had been carved into the three-pronged spiral shape that I recognized from the dead bodies of the wedding killer's victims.

"Black," I said, motioning him over.

He sauntered over to me, barely looking up from his phone.

"Black," I said, more insistently.

When he gave me a vaguely annoyed look, I pointed at the scepter.

He had to have seen it, but he barely gave it a glance before frowning at me, and then turning on his heel and walking away. I stared after him in disbelief, wondering if he didn't know about the spiral patterns carved into the victims found so far.

I know, he told me silently.

He didn't stop walking.

I watched him leave the round exhibit room for the next chamber and then I looked back at the statue myself, studying the three-pronged spiral. Like before, in the morgue with Nick, something about that symbol looked familiar to me, but I had no idea where I'd seen it before. I was sure I'd never encountered this particular sculpture before today.

I knew art a little, and I didn't recognize the name of the artist, either.

The expression on the angel's face appeared hard to me, almost cold. The horse's nostrils flared and it pawed out with one foot, its wings curled and spread more in a war posture than one of flight, especially given the articulation of the angel's streaming robes and upraised arm and outstretched wings. In the hand not holding the scepter, the angel carried a sword.

I'd never seen an image of an angel quite like that one before, not even in the more apocalyptic interpretations of the bible.

The spiral symbol looked a lot more pagan than Christian.

When I asked Black about the piece again, after he walked back through the exhibit hall to collect me, he only shrugged, his eyes back on his phone after a bare glance. I noticed he took a picture of the scepter before we left, however, as well as at least one of what appeared to be a brand carved into the rear of the horse in the same pattern.

"What does it mean?" I persisted. "That symbol?"

He didn't answer.

The look he gave me told me he'd heard me, though. I more got the impression he didn't want to discuss it. Not here.

I stared at the symbol for a few seconds more, maybe just to burn it into my memory. I found myself thinking it might be a distortion of something Celtic, kind of like how the Nazi swastika was a flipped version of a Vedic symbol that could be found all over Europe and Asia for thousands of years. I stared at the spirals long enough to memorize every particular, including the direction of each whorl.

Long enough that Black felt the need to click his fingers at me when he wanted us to leave the downstairs exhibits.

The second time we walked through, he seemed to be looking at the art more, but I got the sense he was comparing the location of every piece to whatever he stared at on his phone's screen...versus looking at the art itself, per se.

I also found myself wondering if he was looking at things like cameras and blind spots, although I never caught him doing it overtly.

When we went out to the courtyard a second time, I sat by the ionic columns, drinking a bottled water I'd gotten from the downstairs café and watching as Black made a few circuits around Rodin's *Thinker*, which stood near the exit overlooking a pool-like fountain. The fountain itself punctuated the center of a circular driveway where tour buses and taxis dropped off passengers, just on the other side of the French-styled pavilion.

I had no idea what he was doing.

While sitting there, however, I found myself thinking that it was an odd coincidence that the inspiration for this museum had come in part from the architecture of the Palace of Fine Arts, where the last murder had taken place. The wife of a wealthy sugar baron had taken a fancy to those French replicas during the World's Fair and asked her husband to build a museum of the same style, which he had done.

I'd forgotten all that, with everything else that happened today.

I was still sitting there, thinking, when Black walked up to me, still gripping his phone in one hand.

"We can go," he informed me.

"You know where he'll stage it?" I said.

"I have an idea," he said cryptically. When I didn't stand up immediately, he just stood there, looming over me and exuding impatience. "I'm hungry," he announced.

Nodding, I pulled myself to my feet, smoothing down the dark coat I wore.

Luckily, in San Francisco, wearing all black didn't make you in the least bit conspicuous. Not in the fall, anyway. Not any time of year, really. Especially not when it looked like rain.

Thinking about that, I glanced up at the sky.

But Black was already walking away from me, his graceful steps purposeful. I watched him disappear through the French-styled archway that led to the stone steps down to the driveway in front of the museum and then to 34th Avenue.

With only the faintest of sighs that time, I followed him.

SEVEN
SPARRING

IT OCCURRED TO ME THAT I'D TURNED MY PHONE OFF.

I'd done it before I left my office.

I guess I had been avoiding having to lie to Nick—overtly, at least. Despite what I told myself earlier, I knew he might call, especially if he was on stakeout in front of Quentin Black's office building and residence.

Especially if he knew I'd been inside. Or that Black had left.

Nick also might do something underhanded, like have Angel call me, which he wasn't above doing. He'd be even more likely to do that since he'd chewed me a new one that morning and might be nervous about how I'd react to him.

I only remembered my phone being off when I slid into a leather booth overlooking the ocean and a glass of red wine was set in front of me.

We were in the upper floor dining room of the Cliff House restaurant, a city landmark and where Black had chosen for us to eat. He claimed the location worked well, being within walking distance of the Legion without being too obviously close. I wasn't exactly sure what that last part meant, but I didn't argue. The Cliff House worked for me since it tended to entertain more tourists than locals given the view and the inflated prices, as well as the long lines from it being a quasi-famous historical site. Not having to fear running into someone I knew appealed to me a lot right then. The last thing I needed was to be seen out dining with Quentin Black, especially with Ian out of town.

Thinking about Ian, I wondered if I should turn the phone back on.

The thought didn't appeal to me truthfully. I remembered Nick's not-so-subtle threat that he might call Ian himself. I wasn't sure if I wanted to know if Nick would really do that to me.

"What are you thinking about?" a voice asked softly.

I looked up, startled, to find Black watching me from across the table.

A faint look of frustration lived in his eyes.

I glanced around us, more in reflex than anything. No one sat particularly close. No one appeared to be looking in our direction either, despite our borderline gothic clothes and Black's strange eyes. Black directed the waitress to lead us to a window table in the corner of the room, which now gradually darkened with the sun setting over the ocean to my right.

It struck me as strange suddenly that Black had given me the corner seat. I would have thought Black to be someone who would want to face the room.

"Mirrors," he said.

I looked back at him.

Then I turned around to look behind me, and realized that a whole collection of mirrors lived on each angle of the corner where I sat, between the long bay window and the window to my left. The booth really should have held a good four or five people, and not only the two of us.

Glancing away from those gold beveled and angel-

118

decorated frames, I looked back at Black, watching as he studied the reflections briefly over my head.

Then he looked back at me, smiling faintly.

"Very discreet," I told him.

"Most people forget about mirrors," he said, leaning back.

"With the added bonus that most won't look at your face in them," I said, thinking aloud. "Or your eyes." I studied his face, folding my fingers on the table in front of me. "You could wear contacts, you know."

"I do sometimes."

"Your face still would stand out."

He looked away from the ocean to meet my gaze.

"Should I take that as a compliment?"

"I don't know," I said, more or less truthfully.

Black's gold eyes reflected light from the setting sun. He went back to looking at the sunset. Or perhaps he only pretended to look as he studied the room in the reflection of the glass. Either way, the sunset light altered the tint of his irises, making them more of a red-gold than the lighter color I remembered from the interrogation room or his apartment.

"So?" He turned, studying my face equally closely. "What were you thinking about? Just then? Or do you not wish to tell me?"

"Nothing," I said.

Then, shaking my head as I realized I was lying, I pulled out my phone, staring at the dead face of it.

"My fiancé, actually. I turned off my phone, and..." I let my words trail, wondering suddenly why I was telling him this. When I glanced up, I saw Black frown, an eyebrow quirked, like he wondered the same thing.

Feeling a glimmer of some other emotion there, I brushed it

away, shaking my head again as if to push that from my mind as well.

"I was trying to decide if I should turn it on," I confessed. "The phone."

"You do not wish to talk to him?"

"Here?" I smiled wryly, looking up. "Not particularly."

"You don't want to lie to him," Black observed.

"No," I said, sighing more genuinely. "I really don't."

"You are trying to decide whether to lie? Or the size of the lie?"

Feeling my face heat as I realized that was pretty much exactly what I'd been doing, I only shook my head.

"I don't know," I said, a little less truthfully.

When the silence stretched, I cleared my throat, glancing around us once more.

"They didn't bring us menus," I said.

"I ordered for us."

I pursed my lips, still clutching the phone in my hands. "You did?"

He leaned deeper into his side of the booth, sighing one of those rumbling sighs of his. "I got you grilled salmon with asparagus, doc. Medium rare. And a salad. Don't worry, it wasn't the Caesar. The apricot gorgonzola. I told them to skip the walnuts, and to put the dressing on the side. I also got us wine. Red for you... even though it will go horribly with the fish."

My jaw loosened. "How the hell could you have possibly known—"

"Lucky guess?"

My mouth shut with a snap.

He quirked an eyebrow at me. "Don't be alarmed, doc. It works better for our cover, does it not? That I seem to be the dutiful boyfriend?" His eyes fell to the ring on my finger. "Or perhaps the dutiful fiancé?"

I leaned closer to him, my hands flat on the table. My voice came out low, but even I heard the threat in it. "All right. I mean it. You're going to talk, Black. Now. Or I'm not going anywhere with you tonight." Seeing his smile begin, I cut him off. "... Anywhere *else,* okay? Moreover, if you keep lying to me, I'll call Nick when I leave here, and tell him everything."

His smile crept back. "Everything, Miriam?"

"Enough to get you picked up tonight... Quentin."

He frowned, opening his mouth to speak.

Again, I didn't give him the chance.

"Since I've already given one of my oldest friends the first real reason to question my word... and my *professional* integrity for that matter, thanks to you... and I'm now contemplating lying to my boyfriend and soon-to-be husband, I think it's time you told me the truth."

Those gold eyes locked with mine. I saw genuine bewilderment there that time.

"The truth about what, Miriam?" he said.

I flinched again when he used my given name.

Then I could only stare at those oddly-opaque gold irises.

Briefly, I saw past the stillness there. I saw enough that I wondered if he *wanted* me to see it, or possibly even to see more of him. Flickers of emotion reached me through the cracks, despite his lack of facial expression—or maybe contrasting that lack to make those flickers more obvious. Realizing I was listening to him—listening hard, for the first time with anyone in as long as I could remember—I bit my lip, partly in frustration at how little I could hear.

I *did* feel things though. Not words, but...

Emotion.

A faint vulnerability. It reminded me of those glimmers of nervousness I got off him when he first invited me into his penthouse apartment. He felt strangely more open in those glimpses, but they were so fleeting, so intangible, I couldn't be sure of anything I felt there, or even if he was planting those impressions on purpose to confuse me.

God, it really felt like...

"You're wasting your time," he said softly.

"Am I?" I retorted. "Because I can feel *something*."

"Not enough," he said. "And nothing relevant to what you seem to want to know."

I stared at him, fighting to think if that felt true. I honestly couldn't decide.

"Are you *letting* me feel those things?" I demanded.

"Which ones?" he said, reweaving his fingers on the table.

"Where it almost feels like you..." I stopped, feeling my face heat. Then I just said it. "It almost feels like you're treating this as a *date*, Mr. Black," I said, my voice curt.

"Are you asking if I'm attracted to you?"

"I'm asking if you're trying to manipulate me," I said, sharper. "Which isn't the same thing. At all."

"No, it isn't," he conceded.

Another silence fell between us.

"So are you letting me feel that? That..." My fingers tightened. "Whatever that is?"

"You know, doc," he said lazily, his eyes giving me a more warning look. "It's rude to try and read me when you could just ask."

"I thought I *was* asking."

"I have yet to hear a coherent question."

"Are you deliberately trying to manipulate me right now?"

"Deliberately?" He raised an eyebrow, smiling faintly. "No."

"But you can't hear me, either?" I said, my frustration audible.

"Correct."

"How can you know so much about me, then?"

He quirked his eyebrow once more, but didn't answer.

"You're not going to tell me?" I said.

"Clearly."

"Why did you let yourself get arrested that morning?" I demanded.

He leaned back, unfolding his hands gracefully as he did, a kind of open-palmed shrug. "What makes you think I did, Miriam?"

I gave him a disparaging look, similar to the ones he'd given me a few times that day. "You can convince a victim's family that they hired you last week, when they'd likely never heard of you before. You can order food without going near a waiter. But you can't do whatever it is you do to convince a bunch of cops to let you go when they find you walking down the street covered in blood?"

"You're making erroneous assumptions," he said, exhaling a bit.

"Which ones?"

"It doesn't work that way here," he said. "It doesn't work here how you're implying. There are... limitations. Risks. I suspect they relate to living around so few of our kind, but all I have are theories at this point. It could be different rules in this dimension compared to our home world. Even different Barrier properties. Either way, I can't do a lot of the things you think I have done. Not here. Not in this dimension."

Pausing, he gave me a more penetrating look.

"It's interesting that you think I can, though, doc. Given that you say you don't remember anything about how you got here."

I stared at him. "I never said that."

He dismissed me with a wave. "It is implied. You don't belong here. You claim you do. Therefore, you don't remember how you got here. Whether or not you believe the stories you were told as a child is utterly irrelevant."

My jaw fell more. "What on Earth is that supposed to mean?"

"Which Earth?" he said, smiling again as he held up his hands. Probably seeing the anger building in my face, he turned his hands into more of a peace gesture. "Relax, doc. Just a little inter-dimensional humor. What I'm telling you is perfectly clear. I can't do a lot of the things you are implying I can do. Not here. That's all you need to understand right now."

"What things?" I said. "With the waiter?"

"I spoke to the waiter by the door," he said. "While you were giving up your coat."

"And the Velaquez's?"

"I had several in my staff talk to them."

"To threaten them?"

He let out a more impatient-sounding sigh. "No. To offer free services if they were willing to testify that they'd hired me last week."

"And they went for that?" I gave him a skeptical look. "They didn't think you were just buying them off because you'd killed their daughter?"

"My people can be very convincing."

I let out a disbelieving snort. "I'll bet." When his expression didn't move, I sharpened my voice. "So you're saying you *couldn't* push those cops to ignore you yesterday morning?"

124

He gave a more noncommittal shrug. "I didn't say that."

"So you could then?"

"Perhaps."

"Then why didn't you?" I said through gritted teeth.

"Perhaps there were too many witnesses."

"At five in the morning?"

He held up his hands in another of those obvious, if odd, shrugs.

"Or maybe you let them arrest you," I said. "Maybe you *wanted* them to arrest you."

"Why on earth would I want that, Miriam?"

"You tell me... Quentin."

There was a silence.

Then he sat all the way back in the leather booth, laying his arm on the top of the backrest.

His eyes had darkened somewhat during our exchange, shifting to a more predatory slant. In the process of leaning back, he removed both hands from the top of the table, resting the one not on the backrest on the booth's seat. I found myself watching the way he moved again, if only for the oddness of his mannerisms and how they flowed. Just another of the dozen or so things about him that were wrong, without my being able to explain to myself *why* they were wrong.

At least, not in a way that made sense.

Adjusting his shoulders and back in the clean but old-looking leather upholstery, he glanced around us at the scattering of other diners, although none of them appeared to be looking at us. Waiters had begun to light candles in the middle of each table as they walked up to take drink orders and dessert orders and to set down plates full of food and refill water and wine glasses.

Thinking over everything I'd asked him, and how few of

my questions he'd actually answered, I looked out at the sunset, wondering again what the hell I was even doing here.

When I glanced back at him, amusement had returned to his eyes.

"You know, I do intend to train you," he said. "Assuming you allow it. But I'm not sure this is the most efficient way to do it, Miriam." He glanced around us. "Or the most discreet."

"Just tell me the truth," I said. "Please. You owe me that."

"Do I?"

"Yes," I said, sharper. "You do. I've come with you on this little jaunt. I'm trusting you... more or less." I lowered my voice more as I leaned over the table towards him. "I'm at least trusting that you won't *murder* me if I go with you tonight, Mr. Black. Which is a lot more trust than anyone I know would place in you. I've taken your word that you aren't really the wedding killer and that this isn't all just some elaborate ruse to make me your next victim. Although the irony that I would have accompanied you while you cased your next killing floor certainly wouldn't be lost on Nick, who might get a kick out of chiseling 'IDIOT' at the top of my headstone..."

Black blinked at that, his eyes showing real surprise.

"You still think that's a possibility?" he said.

"Wouldn't you? If you were me?"

His expression grew thoughtful.

Then he nodded, slowly.

"Yes. I suppose I would." He studied my face, that predatory glint returning to his eyes, making them look more animal-like again. "Does that mean you aren't coming with me tonight, doc? Because I confess, that would be... disappointing."

I watched him look at me, seeing that warier look sharpen.

He still didn't frighten me though.

Honestly, the realization almost frustrated me.

"I didn't say that," I said after another pause, even as I wondered *why* I wasn't saying that. I glanced around us before I lowered my voice. "My point is, you say you want me to come. You seem to even mean it. So if I go with you, that makes this a favor, at least in part."

He lifted his eyebrow. "Does it? I'm not sure I agree."

"I don't care if you agree. It's a favor. And I want a favor in return."

"Which is...?"

"Information," I said tersely. "Why did you let the police pick you up?"

When he didn't answer right away, I fought with another jaw-clenching rush of anger, intense enough that it startled me, even as the more clinical side of my brain noted how unusual that was for me these days.

I didn't usually get this emotional. Not anymore. Not even with Ian.

It also made me wonder if Black was doing that to me too, intentionally or not.

Remembering how I'd been as a child didn't help, or how my father threatened me with a psychologist of my very own if I didn't learn how to control my violent outbursts.

Zoe helped me with that, too. It was sort of ironic, given what I did for a living now.

I hadn't thought about any of that in years, though.

I refocused on Black with an effort. "Tell me why you're *really* doing all of this. And why you let yourself get picked up for murder, when I'm pretty sure you could have walked away unseen that morning. Even covered in blood."

He frowned at me again.

That time, however, I could see him thinking on the other side of that frown.

Meanwhile, I was going over my previous words in my head, and realizing some of them sounded a lot more plausible out loud than they had when I'd just been thinking them.

Maybe this museum trip really was just an elaborate set up.

Maybe I really was the idiot Nick thought me to be, at least when it came to Black.

It had already been pointed out to me by both Nick and Black that I fit the wedding killer's victim profile. Professional woman, twenties to early thirties. Athletic build. Long hair.

Engaged to be married.

Black seemed to feel at least a hint of where my head was going. Making that strange clicking sound, he leaned closer to me, until his gold eyes met mine from only a few inches away. I didn't flinch back, but it took an effort, if only for the intensity that lived there.

"I'm not here to kill you, Miriam," he murmured. "On the contrary, I would protect you with my life."

I studied his expression from up close, a little thrown by the deadly seriousness there.

"...But I realize my saying so probably won't reassure you," he added, moving back somewhat. "Especially since I would likely say the same thing if I did intend to kill you." He studied my eyes again, that frown touching the corners of his sculpted lips. Then he seemed to make up his mind. When he did, he finally leaned all the way back into the booth.

I exhaled a breath I hadn't known I held.

"I did let myself get picked up," he said, blunt.

I flinched a third time. Then I pursed my lips.

"Why?" I said.

He exhaled, staring out the window at the now blood-red clouds.

The sky was almost entirely dark apart from those splashes of color and an indigo and gold line at the level of the horizon. Looking back at me, he seemed to make up his mind a second time, maybe to go all the way with this. Or maybe only to convince me he'd decided that. I found myself thinking that, in addition to everything else, he might be skilled at throwing out emotions that he may or may not actually feel.

He smiled even as I thought it, right before he made another of those oddly graceful gestures with one hand, resting it back on top of the table.

"There were several reasons," he said.

"Like what?"

"I was tracking this rogue, as I said. I'd just determined, more or less definitively, that he was murdering humans in a brutal way. And that he was ritualizing it."

I narrowed my eyes, hearing the emotion in his voice for the first time when he spoke about the murders. He'd sounded genuinely angry.

Disgusted, at least.

"Because of that," he continued, making another smooth gesture with his hand. "I wanted more information about where the cops were with the case. I considered pushing those beat cops to not see me," he added more softly, glancing around us as if to make sure we weren't being overheard. "But I knew that was risky. Then I thought, why not let them bring me in? It might prove an interesting exercise. And it did."

"Why not just show up in the waiting area to read the cops as they walked past?" I said. "Or at the corner coffee shop, for that matter? Why bother being arrested?"

He smiled, but it didn't touch his eyes.

Rather, they grew deadly serious again.

"One of the things I will apparently need to teach you, Miriam, is that it is very difficult to find a good reason to sit inside a police station and stare into space for numerous minutes, without responding when people attempt to speak with you," he said.

He continued to study my face. Briefly, I got the strangest impression he saw himself as genuinely educating me just then, despite the sarcasm.

"...Also, as I have told you repeatedly now, it doesn't work that way here. In-depth reads take considerably more work in this dimension, Miriam. It is much, much faster to do that work when you can guide the direction of your subject's thoughts. Or, failing that, when you allow yourself to be interrogated about the very subject about which you require information."

Leaning deeper into the booth, he sighed one of those purring sighs of his.

"You learn how to hide what you are, when you operate the kind of business I do," he said. "I can't hide behind the nonverbal language and deception detection training you can claim as a psychologist. Not nearly as convincingly, at least. Your gender and sexuality probably disarm a number of male humans as well. A valuable tactic, but not a reliable one."

I felt my jaw harden, but said nothing, in part because I distinctly got the impression that he was trying to get a reaction out of me.

"Further," he added after that pause. "...I'm tracking a rogue *seer*, as I said. I don't know his exact relationship with the human authorities, but it's not beyond the realm of imagination that he might have an interest in how the investigation is proceeding, particularly on a morning he'd just committed a crime. For all I knew, he had direct connections in the station. Which means, there is some chance he would pick up on *me* if I spied openly. The same risk pertained to tracking individual detectives. I don't know what kinds of resources this seer has at his disposal. Or what kind of protection he has. Including psychic protection—"

"Seer?" I interrupted, staring at him. "You said that twice. That's what you call them?"

"Yes." His gaze flickered over me briefly. "That is what I call *us*, Miriam."

"You said 'he' again?" I pressed.

"Statistical probability."

I let that slide, thinking over the rest of his words. "You don't want this 'rogue' or whatever it is to know you're following him?" I said.

"Correct." He made another vague gesture with one hand. "Obviously." After a pause, he tilted his head in a different kind of gesture. That one seemed almost apologetic. "I was also in need of a forensic psychologist, as I said."

I stared. Then my eyes abruptly narrowed to slits. "What?"

Sighing a bit, he pulled out his smart phone. Tapping in a few keys and sliding his fingers across the front several times, he turned the screen around then, showing it to me.

Filling the screen was the headline and cover photo of a webzine article. The picture stood beneath blood-red text that shouted "NURSERY KILLER CAUGHT IN SOUTH BAY." I knew the photo and scowled. In it, I stood behind Nick, wearing a taut expression and a bullet proof vest, my arms folded in front of my chest, my hair back in a ponytail. It was from Nick's last big publicity case, outside the house of the suspect I'd found for him.

"Nasty piece of work, that one," Black said, squinting down at the image of me on the small screen. "Little boys, was it?"

My fingers clenched in my lap. "You knew who I was? Before yesterday?"

"Not in the way you mean. But I was... intrigued."

"And you knew they would bring me in to talk to you?"

"I knew it was a distinct possibility. More precisely, I knew that your boy, Tanaka, was assigned to this case... and that if I was uncooperative enough, he might feel inspired to improvise. I also happened to know your office was located down the street."

A smile touched my lips, but it didn't contain any humor.

"You must know how ludicrous that sounds," I told him.

"Why?" he said, throwing up his hands gracefully. "I was in need of a forensic psychologist. You were being touted as a 'miracle worker.' I like to recruit from the best in the field." He paused, once again looking at the image of me on the screen. "And I may not have known *what* you were, doc, but I knew you weren't what you were pretending to be."

"Which is what?" I retorted.

"Harmless," he said at once. Glancing at me, he tapped the photo with one finger. "I can see a lot in photos, doc. More than you'd believe."

"I have office hours," I said, gritting my teeth.

He shrugged. "I like to assess people in their element when I meet them. Even from just one photo, you struck me as a field worker type. Not a clinician. As much as you tried to hide that fact with your posture in this photo."

"Really? What gave me away?"

"Your eyes. Which are positively stunning, by the way." He gave me a faint smile. Before I could react, he showed me the image again, and tapped where my hand rested by the edge of

132

the flak jacket. "Oh... and the gun. Did your pal Tanaka know you were packing heat that night? I know he didn't know you read that pedophile to find the booby-traps he left all over the house. I imagine that took some creativity on your part, to implant that idea without him suspecting." He gave me a look containing an open flicker of disgust. "That couldn't have been fun, either. Being inside that particular mind. I'm amazed you didn't shoot him on sight."

I swallowed, wanting to argue with him.

I didn't, though.

He gave another of those graceful shrugs. "What better way to assess your skills than to see what you could make of me? Then I felt you trying to read me from inside that glass booth..." His jaw hardened, right before he gave me an openly heated look. "*Gaos*, doc... I admit, I got a hard on in about two seconds when I felt that. And again, when I couldn't get past your shield. I can't even begin to tell you what a wholly unexpected and welcome surprise that was..."

When I averted my gaze, I heard him smile.

He made another of those shrugging gestures and I glanced back at him, my eyes following his hand and fingers.

"I'm not buying this shy act either, doc. Although I might believe the confusion." He shook his head, smiling as he looked out the window. "...And no, I don't believe it's a coincidence, you being here," he added, softer. "Not with that rogue here. Not with me here, for that matter." Turning, he met my gaze seriously. "I'm not always here, you know... in San Francisco. Even with my main office here, I'm often... elsewhere."

That hard, predatory look rose in his eyes as he studied my face.

"You have no idea just how truly *rare* our kind is in this

dimension, doc," he said. "We'd be on the critically endangered species list... if humans knew about us at all." He glanced down at my ring finger. "And apart from your race, you fit his victim profile. Which I find... interesting. Just like your friend, Naoko Tanaka, finds it interesting."

I fought another wave of confusion, again feeling something about him threatening my more clinical veneer. I tried to decide if I wanted to follow him down his whole "other race" rabbit hole. Even though I'd started this, I decided I didn't. Not here. Not now.

"You really think he's targeting me?" I said. "The wedding killer?"

He continued to stare out the window, not answering at first.

Then he shrugged, leaning back to level that predatory stare at me again.

"I honestly don't know." He exhaled, leaning deeper in the leather booth. "What do you think, doc? Or do you still believe this is all just one big coincidence? An astrological convergence of sorts, with you and I at the center?"

Before I could answer, the waiter appeared with my salad.

The waiter set it down in front of me, along with a full glass of red wine that I hadn't ordered. Ignoring the salad, I found myself picking up the thin-stemmed glass before the waiter had even left the table with my old one. I took a few good swallows of what turned out to be a different bottle, this time a better than decent merlot. I'd just set the glass down by my plate when my gaze for some reason flickered towards the bar.

Once it had, I did a double-take, then felt myself pale.

"What?" Black said.

I glanced from the bar to him, but he was already focusing his stare on the mirrors hanging on the wall behind me. I contemplated getting up, rising quickly to my feet, perhaps thinking to head both of them off, or maybe to walk to the other end of the bar before the person sitting there saw me sitting in the corner booth with Black.

I was too late, though.

The person at the bar had already seen me.

He was already sliding off his stool and then he was walking directly towards me.

"What, Miriam?" Black said, still not turning around. "Who is that?"

"It's Ian," I said, feeling light-headed as I watched my fiancé walk towards our corner booth with a smile on his handsome face.

Picking up my glass, I took a really big swallow of the merlot, setting the tulip-shaped glass down as I rose shakily to my feet.

I found myself conscious suddenly of the borrowed clothes I was wearing.

"He's here," I said numbly.

YOU ARE THE ABSOLUTE *WORST* PERSON TO SURPRISE IN HUMAN history," Ian smiled, grasping my elbow as he leaned closer to kiss my cheek. "...The absolute worst."

I forced a smile. My eyes drifted down to Black as I accepted the kiss. He hadn't stood up when Ian reached our table and now I found myself noticing the faint air of hostility drifting off Black as he watched Ian kiss me. As for me, I was deeply aware

135

I was probably ten different shades of guilty-looking even as I tried to shake the feeling off.

Whatever I was doing here, it was no threat to Ian.

I desperately wanted to believe that, anyway.

"Sorry," I murmured, my face still uncomfortably hot. "You caught me on kind of a strange night." I motioned towards Black, not looking down at him as I studied Ian's face. "I'd like you to meet Quentin Black," I said, deciding to tell him part of the truth at least. "He's a new prospective employer," I added. "He runs a private investigation and security firm downtown and wants me to consider a possible job with his permanent staff."

Ian raised his eyebrows subtly, keeping that humor on his face.

Even so, he appeared to be studying my expression more closely than usual. I was about to speak again when he glanced down at Black, barely hesitating before he extended a hand.

"Ian Stone," he said, smiling.

"You're British," Black observed, rising smoothly to his feet.

The way he towered over Ian felt strangely deliberate.

Ian's hardly short. At roughly six foot even, he's well above average.

I hadn't thought to hazard a guess about Black's exact height until then. Looking at the two of them together however, I thought: *Six-five? Six-six?*

"Yes," Ian said, his lips quirking in what might have been amusement as he gazed up at Black's face, obviously tracking the way he was using his height as well. "This surprises you?"

"No," Black said at once, glancing at me. "Actually, it explains some of Ms. Fox's speech patterns. At times she uses phrasing more from your home country than her own."

Ian glanced at me in another silent question.

136

Without waiting for my answer, he looked back at Black, right before releasing his hand.

"You *are* a detective, aren't you?" Ian teased, his voice still holding mainly friendliness and humor. "I suppose it shouldn't surprise me that you'd notice such a thing. Still, I imagine Miri finds it entertaining... compared to her usual sorts of clients. Most of those are a bit on the boring side, in terms of companies. Isn't that right, darling?"

I smiled, shaking my head. "According to you, all business people are dull, Ian. Which is sort of ironic given what you do for a living..."

"Which is what... precisely?" Black said, narrowing his gaze at Ian.

Ian gave him a wry smile.

"Well, I could tell you, but then I'd have to kill you," he said, causing me to let out an involuntary laugh. "And if you meant to flatter me by implying Miri's picked up my speech mannerisms due to her fondness for me... or to reassure me perhaps, given that I've just caught my fiancée out drinking wine with a man I've never met... I have to commend you for being cleverer than most of her clients, too."

I was used to Ian's humor, so his words didn't really surprise me.

I heard the faint edge there, however, which did surprise me a little.

Ian didn't normally bother sparring with other men in social situations, certainly not over me. Both of us were pretty laid back about the trust thing; we had been almost from the beginning. I hadn't really seen Ian spar with other men over anything else either, come to think of it. Not in a social situation, at least. He tended to reserve that for his work.

137

Ian was confident, which was one of the things I liked about him.

Even as I thought it, I found myself thinking Ian was measuring Black more closely than I'd ever seen him look at anyone, even at the few work functions of his I'd attended.

Weirder still, he seemed to be trying to hide it.

Was he really threatened? Had he seen me and Black talking and picked up on something? I'd never given Ian a single reason not to trust me, but he was only human.

And Black was...

Well, handsome wasn't the right word.

But if I saw Ian with a female equivalent to Black, I would definitely feel threatened.

Truthfully though, I'm much more the jealous type than Ian is. Maybe it was related to that emotional volatility that I'd struggled with as a kid, but I really had to work sometimes to keep it in check, especially with how often Ian traveled and how secretive he could be due to his job. I trusted my boyfriend, like I said, but I'd always had issues with being possessive.

Ian usually seemed completely immune to such things. He claimed it was because he trusted me absolutely, but I suspected a lot of it was just temperament.

But now? Looking at him, I honestly couldn't be sure.

I never read Ian though. Never.

Boyfriends were even more of a hard line than friends, when it came to the psychic stuff.

I never violated their minds. For any reason.

Even as I thought it, Black glanced at me, his sculpted lips quirking as he slid his hands into his pockets. His whole energy changed as he did it. Moreover, it was the first time I'd seen him put his hands in his pockets at all. It was a strangely "normal" gesture for him, and kind of threw me since I hadn't seen him do a lot of normal things in the short period I'd known him.

Watching him interact with Ian, it struck me suddenly that both of them appeared to be wearing costumes.

"Sorry," Black said, rocking slightly on his heels, another normal-ish thing to do I hadn't seen him do until then. "The detective thing can be hard to shut off. Miriam told me you were traveling for business? You've just returned from Bangkok, am I right?"

I looked at Black again, sharper than I should have.

I had no memory of telling him where Ian had gone.

"Yes," Ian said, smiling, his own hands now in his pockets.

"Do you like it there?" Black asked politely.

I noticed his gold eyes sharpened slightly after he asked it.

Ian shrugged, glancing at me before he smiled up at Black. "It has its charms. The food is quite good. It has some stunning rooftop views. And I do enjoy haggling in the markets."

Black nodded, but I found myself wondering if he was even listening.

Further, the nodding, the way he held his body, the hands in his pockets... all of it was throwing me off balance, if only because he came off as a totally different person than the one I'd been sitting with just a few minutes earlier.

Ian seemed to be measuring Black with his eyes, too.

"You need her for long?" he inquired politely. "I've only just got back, as I said. I'd hoped to surprise her at her flat, once I finished here."

I frowned slightly, looking back towards the bar.

For the first time, it occurred to me to wonder why Ian was here.

"Client's just left, darling," Ian explained, following the

direction of my stare. Smiling, he looked back at Black. "Well? Should I wait? Or is it to be a long night for you two?"

"At least a few hours, I'm afraid," Black said. "Possibly more. I apologize, given the circumstances, but I'd really hoped to get her to sign a preliminary consulting contract tonight, if possible. And to check out one of the suspects in the case I'm working before he can skip town."

He gave Ian another strangely business-normal smile, like they were old frat buddies.

"...It really can't wait until tomorrow," he added, and I noticed for the first time that the odd, difficult-to-identify accent of his had vanished too, leaving only nondescript American businessman. "I am sorry. But this suspect is a serious flight risk. The window is short."

Ian's own smile didn't waver. "Of course," he said. "I completely understand. I have a few things I could be taking care of myself tonight, anyway."

"Why are you back early?" I asked Ian.

Ian glanced at me, and from the look on his face, I wondered if my question was overly blunt. "I missed you," he said, smiling in a rueful way. "They didn't need me, and after our conversation yesterday, I thought perhaps I should bow out early if I could."

I felt my face heat as his words sank in.

"Oh." My surprise turned swiftly into guilt. "I'm sorry."

"Completely my fault. I can't surprise people and change my schedule without telling them, only to be angry when they aren't available."

There was a silence between the three of us. It felt dense that time.

Then Ian smiled wider at Black. "Mind if I borrow her for a few? Before giving her up for the evening?"

Black gave a strange sort of bow, but again, something about it carried more of a regular joe business guy vibe than the alien-type body movements of his I'd noted before.

"Of course," he said. He smiled a 100-watt smile after he said it.

I couldn't help staring at him, noting the differences, until I felt Ian's eyes on me. Then I turned, smiling at him as normally as I could.

"Shall we?" I said, angling my body away from the corner booth.

Ian nodded, motioning for me to lead the way, which I did.

When I glanced back, I saw Ian and Black measuring one another a last time before a final handshake. Seeing the flat look in Ian's eyes, I found myself thinking that my soon-to-be husband was as good of an actor as Black.

I couldn't decide how I felt about that, truthfully.

EIGHT
BAD GIRLFRIEND

R ATHER THAN TO THE BAR, IAN LED ME TO THE FRONT DOOR OF THE
Cliff House restaurant.

He waited for the hostess to get my coat from the back, taking it from her when she returned and handed it to him with a flirtatious smile. He rolled his eyes at my irritated snort, smiling at me tautly before he held the coat up for me to put on.

"Is this new?" Ian murmured, as I slid my arms into the sleeves.

I felt myself flush, but kept my back to him as I answered. "I left mine at home today, so I picked one up downtown."

"It's nice. A bit on the clandestine side."

I let out a laugh, looking up at him. "What does that mean?"

"You could be a spy in that coat."

"You would know," I murmured.

"Indeed I would."

I smiled. Even so, I found myself wondering again, just how long Ian had been there at the bar while Black and I had been talking.

It wasn't like Ian to spar with me, either.

He didn't say anything else until we'd walked outside. Even

then, he walked me a dozen paces away from the restaurant, leading me by the hand up the sidewalk until we were on a section of dirt pathway overlooking the Sutro Baths. Nothing more than a ruin of a stone foundation remained of the baths themselves, nestled in a small bay below the southern edge of Land's End.

Looking back at the lit up restaurant and the dark ocean behind it, I took in the panorama in a quick sweep of my eyes, strangely conscious of Black, even out here.

Once Ian had me on the apex of that windswept segment of sandy path, he released my hand. He turned on me, his blue eyes suddenly sharp, and completely devoid of humor.

"Where have you been, Miri?" he demanded, his voice holding an edge. "I've been worried. I've also been calling. For hours now."

Studying his face, I understood now, why I'd picked up so much weirdness on him.

He'd been posturing in front of Black all right. Not because he'd been threatened by Black himself, but because he'd been annoyed with me.

The wind whipped at my cheeks and eyes, forcing me to look away. I held my hair back with one hand, tugging it under the collar of the dark coat.

"Ian, I'm sorry, really. I turned my phone off and forgot. You know I'm prone to forgetting my phone... and I had no idea you were coming home tonight, so I wasn't expecting a call until tomorrow."

That part was true at least.

It didn't smooth any of the tension from Ian's face.

"Don't play games with me, Miri," he said, his voice colder. "Nick called me."

I sighed, silently swearing to myself I was going to kill Nick Tanaka.

"...something about a serial killer who's obsessed with you? He seemed to think the guy was his wedding killer. He also said he might have to let him go today." His voice grew harder, even as he pointed down the hill towards the Cliff House. "What the hell are you doing out with a *client,* given that? You're aware you fit the victim profile, yes? That you're the type of woman this 'wedding killer' likes to target? Nick made it sound like his suspect was practically salivating over you..."

"Ian..." I sighed.

"Don't 'Ian' me," he snapped. "I'm not Nick. I know when you're playing naive because you think the rest of us are too stupid to know it's an act. What happened in that interrogation room yesterday? I could tell Nick didn't share everything."

I shook my head, tugging my hair out of my face again when some of it pulled free of my collar. Pressing my lips together, I met his gaze.

"Nick is being ridiculously paranoid about me, Ian," I said. "I *told* him as much, both times I talked to him about it. That guy he had me interview? He was playing games, it's true. And maybe he was a little too excited when a woman went in there to interrogate him, but that had nothing to do with me." The lie felt bitter on my tongue, but I did my best to keep it off my face, to keep my voice bored. "Honestly, I'm still not convinced Nick has the real killer. He kicked me off the case anyway, didn't he tell you?"

"No," Ian said, frowning at me harder.

I held his gaze, watching him assess my expression.

I knew he did it partly in reflex, but it made me tense anyway. That was the problem with dating someone whose job required

145

them to read micro-expressions all the time, and who knew how to hide their reactions from view.

Normally I had less reason to be paranoid about it.

Normally, I wasn't lying to him.

He sighed, even as I thought it. "I'm sorry for being alarmist. Nick got my dander up, I admit. Had me worried you were tied up in a trunk somewhere."

"What the hell did he say to you?" I said, letting him hear my annoyance.

"Too much. And not enough," Ian said. Combing a hand through his hair, he exhaled hard again, sounding faintly angry. "I was about to get on a twenty-hour flight so I couldn't even talk to him, at least not enough to get the whole story. I suppose I could have called him back once the plane was in the air, but I figured since there wasn't much I could do about it en route..." He trailed, glancing at me with a frown. "I got enough to know Nick was worried about you last night. Worried enough to contact me in Bangkok, even though he must have known you'd be furious at him for that."

At my sympathetic sound, he stepped closer, his voice tense.

"Miri, he made it sound like he really thought you were at risk. I've never heard him like that before. Not about you. And you two have done cases like this before."

"Well... not *exactly* like this," I said, smiling.

Ian wasn't mollified. "He was worried enough that he told me he intended to keep you under surveillance until they had this chap to rights, Miri," he said. "He was going to put a tail on you, if he ended up having to let his suspect walk."

I fought to keep the reaction off my face.

Clearly Ian had no idea that Quentin Black was the suspect Nick had been talking about.

Which meant he'd never gotten a name from Nick.

Still studying my face, Ian sighed, letting go of my arm.

"Okay, so I might have overreacted a bit, when I couldn't get ahold of you," he said, combing his fingers through his sandy blond — and now windswept — hair. His thick and usually near-perfect hair remained sticking up somewhat when he finished, probably because he hadn't gotten a shower since the flight.

"I *am* sorry, Miri," he said. "To be honest, I panicked a little when I didn't find you at your flat. I had your phone traced. I was on the verge of dialing Nick when I saw you in that booth. I only hesitated earlier because I knew you might *kill* me if it turned out you were out with Lacey having drinks."

"You had my phone traced?" I said in disbelief.

He nodded, his expression sheepish. "Yes." He gave me a slightly defensive look. "It was the first time, Miri. I swear it. I was afraid for your life."

Deciding to let it go, I walked closer to him, rubbing his arm through the jacket.

"I'm so sorry," I said, and meant it. "You must be exhausted."

He let out a low laugh. "I am. That damned negotiation was brutal. The Bangkok thing, I mean. Positively brutal." He glanced down at me, smiling faintly. "So you really have to be with this P.I. fellow tonight? I was hoping for a foot massage... and some wine. Maybe a lot of wine. Along with a massage of a few other body parts."

I let out a low laugh, stepping closer so that I was between his arms. When he wrapped them around me, I rubbed his back through the dress shirt.

"You still mad at me for being gone too much?" he said.

I shook my head, snuggling deeper into his arms.

"You sure?"

"I'm sure. But ask me tomorrow." I paused. "Have you been home yet?"

"Only long enough to dump my bags," he said, sighing again. "And finish geo-locating my fiancée's phone." Despite his embarrassment, I felt him relaxing as I continued to massage the small of his back with my fingers. He looked down at me again. "I really did try to call first, Miri... before I resorted to spyware. Ten times, at least. You might find a few panicked messages from me if you ever bother to turn your phone on again."

I nodded, feeling another wave of guilt as I bit my lip.

I found myself wavering too, wondering if I should tell Ian who Black was, what I'd been doing all day. I'd never kept anything important from him before. He wrapped his arm around me tighter while I was still thinking, squeezing me against his side.

"This new client of yours," Ian grunted when I coiled my own arm tighter around his waist under the long coat. "He's not ugly enough for how I'm feeling right now, either, pet."

I let out a laugh, smacking him lightly in the chest. "Is that jealousy? Seriously? Because I might need to pull out my phone and record it, if so. It might be a first."

"I might actually be worried if you bothered to turn on your phone at all," he grumbled.

I held him tighter, pressing my face against his chest.

Again I tried to decide if I should tell him who he'd just met inside the Cliff House. I knew he'd find out eventually. It was inevitable now. He would eventually hear Black's name from Nick or in the news, and since Ian tended to have a pretty close to photographic memory when it came to names and faces, he would put two and two together. It was part of Ian's job to remember people like he did; he'd told me that more than once.

148

I was more or less the same way, if for different reasons. Even so, Ian's attention to detail still managed to awe me at times.

But I knew I was still avoiding.

The problem was, if I told Ian who Black was, the first thing he'd do is call Nick.

The second thing he'd do is blow a gasket at me for putting myself at risk.

I definitely wouldn't be going anywhere else with Black that night.

I'd also caught the double meaning in some of what Black said to Ian. He really thought there was a "flight risk" with the killer. Maybe he even thought this could be our last chance to catch him. Which meant that if Black was right and the killer really was a psychic—in the sense of being the kind of psychic Black was himself—then he'd probably get away. Even if I told Nick to stake out the Legion of Honor tonight in our place, the cops wouldn't be able to catch someone like that, not without help from someone like Black.

And could I really defend what I'd been doing that day? The storyline itself was more or less coherent—in terms of finding Black at home unexpectedly when I'd really only intended to check out his business—but that did zero to explain my motives, or why I would go with Black after Nick explicitly warned me to stay away from him.

Besides, I knew Ian. I knew how crazy all of this would sound to someone as hyper-rational as Ian was, even apart from his intelligence training.

To Nick and his cop brain, it wouldn't just sound crazy. It would sound complicit.

I was ninety percent certain Nick would simply arrest me, probably for obstructing justice. He'd definitely think I'd been lying to him about my prior knowledge of Black and the nature of our relationship. Assuming he wasn't convinced of that already.

Thinking about that, I sighed again.

Nick *did* think that already. I was kidding myself to believe otherwise.

So really, the issue was Ian.

Either way, I'd be gambling on whether Ian would forgive me for lying to him about who Black was. Given that I'd never talked to Ian about the psychic thing before, that might open a whole can of worms that could bleed into our relationship for a long time after.

As I thought about that end of things, I felt a harder pain, deeper in my chest.

That was the larger part of this that I'd been avoiding. That part, I'd been avoiding for months... well before I'd ever heard the name Quentin Black.

Namely, was it fair to let Ian marry me without telling him what a freak his wife-to-be truly was? Somehow, meeting Black had caused me to question my decision to remain quiet on that front all over again. Maybe it wasn't as small a part of me as I liked to pretend. Maybe it really wasn't fair not to tell Ian about it before we tied the knot for real.

Now that Ian had seen me with Black, I would have to decide. I would have to decide what I would tell him when I got caught... which would definitely happen.

It was just a matter of when.

A part of me still wanted to hold that moment off, however.

At least until after we caught the wedding killer.

Remembering everything Black had told me, I felt that desire to wait on telling Ian intensify. I'd never met anyone like me before. A few crackpots who claimed psychic powers, sure.

A few people who could read a little bit, like that witchy woman who glimpsed what I was behind my shield.

But no one like Black. No one anywhere near what he was.

A part of me just couldn't let it go.

I also found myself thinking that however this thing played out, it would definitely point me in one direction or the other in terms of how much to tell Ian about what and who I really was.

"So?" Ian said, shaking me gently. "Can you get out of this thing? Claim fiancé emergency and reschedule? You can call me a twat, if it helps. Claim I'm a needy, clingy fucker who's jealous you're out with another man on his first night back in town in two weeks..."

"Because that would completely help in selling my credibility to a prospective employer," I said, laughing a little as I gave him a mock frown.

"You know I'm kidding," he said softer, holding me tighter. "I'm serious about the rescheduling though. Any chance you can get out of this thing? Just for tonight?"

Ian was one of the smartest people I knew.

Maybe that's why I was never dumb enough to lie to him usually.

As if he'd heard me, he exhaled again. "You can't, can you?"

I made my decision before I knew I meant to.

I shook my head. "Can't do it. Sorry."

He frowned, but I saw no surprise in his eyes. "Yeah. I figured, based on what he said. Thought it couldn't hurt to grovel a bit, though."

I shook him back, still hugging him around the waist. "Anyway, you should get some sleep. Go home and take a bath and crash." I hesitated, glancing up at him with a smile. "I'll come by in the morning with bagels and coffee. I can give you that, err... massage... then, too. When we're both a bit more up for it."

He grinned, making his dimple stand out and making me feel guilty all over again.

"Okay," he said, sighing more theatrically as he released me. "Well, I guess I'd better go. Your Mr. Quentin Black will think I've stolen you. And I'm seriously about to drop."

"You stink a bit, too," I informed him.

He laughed, shoving at my shoulder with a hand as we made our way back down the path to the sidewalk. When I reached his side by the row of parked cars, he caught hold of my arms, pulling me against him. Before I could speak, he crushed me in his arms, kissing me hard on the mouth. He tasted like whiskey and garlic, which didn't bother me but shocked me a bit before I fell into the kiss, sliding an arm around his neck as I kissed him back. He pulled me tight up against him as he kissed me a second time.

When he stopped, he leaned his forehead against mine.

"I really did miss you, Miri," he murmured.

I closed my eyes, nuzzling his face as I felt a denser tug of guilt. "I missed you, too. Now go get some sleep so I can show you how much tomorrow."

"Why do I feel like I'm being dismissed?" he said with a smile.

"Because you are," I retorted, smiling as I released him. I smacked him on the ass with my palm. "Now go. You're distracting me. And this guy pays well."

"Aye, ma'am."

As Ian walked away, heading up the road to where I now saw his parked SUV, I fought another twinge of guilt, watching as he hit the clicker to unlock the doors. I waited for him to open the door and climb into the driver's seat before I turned, aiming my feet back down the hill and towards the Cliff House bar and restaurant.

"I'm a bad girlfriend," I muttered under my breath.

I told myself it was all right, that at base Ian trusted me, that I'd be able to make this right with him in the end, even if he was furious with me when he found out I'd lied to him about Black. I wasn't cheating on him.

I wasn't betraying our relationship, even if I wasn't including him in this thing.

But it wasn't all right.

I knew damned well it wasn't right, that I was crossing a big line for the two of us. It was a line I would never have dreamed of crossing before today.

Worse, I couldn't even fully explain to myself *why* I was crossing it.

For the first time, I'd given Ian reason to doubt me.

Quentin Black had managed in less than twenty-four hours what hadn't happened to me and Ian once in over a year: I'd lied to my fiancé. I'd given Ian cause to doubt my word. Glancing up at the Cliff House sign as I approached the heavy wooden door, I exhaled again.

Worse than that, there was something between me and Black.

I knew it, even as I tried to convince myself it wasn't true.

And while I didn't see it as a threat to me and Ian—at least not in the usual man and woman sense—I knew it also wasn't only the psychic thing. It wasn't only that we were both looking for the wedding killer either, or that seeing that girl in the morgue somehow dredged up memories of the murder of my baby sister, Zoe.

It was more than that.

More than I wanted to think about, truthfully. Or even acknowledge.

There was something else there — some kind of *connection* between Black and me — although I couldn't for the life of me decide what it meant.

Black's explanation for that bond was absurd of course. Ludicrous.

Even so, his crazy theories about inter-dimensional races didn't negate the bond itself.

Nor did it do anything to help the nearly compulsive quality I felt behind it, at least in regards to me. It was almost like I couldn't help myself around him. I couldn't seem to force myself to *want* to stay away from him.

Which my clinical brain told me probably meant Black was a psychopath.

The more I thought about that, the more something else became abundantly clear.

I should leave.

I should march right back up that sidewalk and try to flag down Ian before he drove away. That, or I should walk to Geary Street on my own and grab a bus or a cab back to my place, or even downtown to pick up my car from that parking garage. Hell, I could call a cab right here, have them take me to the police station on Fillmore so I could tell Nick everything that happened over the last six or seven hours.

Then I could call Ian, apologize profusely and beg for his forgiveness — right before I went over there with his favorite take-out Chinese, a few bottles of good red wine and a hell of a lot of massage oil.

I wouldn't need to give Quentin Black another thought.

But I knew I wasn't going to do any of that.

I knew I wouldn't even before I'd finished unbuttoning the front of that borrowed coat, standing at the door of the Cliff House restaurant.

Even so, I stood there for a few seconds longer, pretending like I might.

NINE
BREAKING
AND ENTERING

WE WALKED THROUGH THE TREES WITHOUT TALKING.
Only the whisper of branches made any sound, along with the occasional call of an owl or a much more high-pitched sonic ping of a bat. I also heard sounds that I assumed had to be feral cats scuffling and looking for food...or possibly raccoons, which I knew lived in pockets all through the more wooded areas of the city.

I barely tracked those things as we walked.

I found I was on high alert already, even though I could only see the barest glow of lights around the Legion of Honor in the distance.

I was wearing the bullet proof vest Black had given me in his office, the same one he'd stuffed in a canvas bag before we got in the helicopter.

We'd retrieved everything out of the trunk of that hatchback car with blacked out windows we'd left parked on a side lot of the VA hospital complex. The lot where Black's employees left the car had few streetlights at night, I learned. It was also lined with trees, and stood close to the beginnings of the path that would lead us into the back end of the park around the Legion of Honor. In addition to the equipment Black had given me, the bags held Black's own guns of course, and a collection of knives that made me nervous when Black first uncovered them.

Other things in the hatchback included ammunition magazines and that third, much heavier black canvas bag, the one I didn't ask too many questions about back at his office. Given its obvious weight and larger size, I suspected it contained larger capacity magazines and possibly larger weapons.

It turned out I was more or less right about both.

Flashbacks hit me inexplicably every few minutes now, mainly to the hills of Afghanistan despite the vastly different terrain.

I suspected the big guns had something to do with it.

More and more, this felt like a military operation, not a private investigator's snooping.

For the same reason, my nerves ratcheted higher with each step we took.

At least I wasn't carrying one of those heavier weapons myself.

Black, on the other hand, wore some kind of high-tech short rifle on a strap under his long coat—something I confess I wasn't familiar with at all, and might have been custom-made. In addition to the modified rifle, he wore at least three handguns I'd seen him slot into holsters, as well as a long knife stuck in an upside-down sheath from which an ivory handle curved outwards at the small of his back.

I suspected he had more than what I saw.

I didn't ask, but my eyes were pretty wide by the time he finished gearing up.

I also checked my own two handguns about four times while watching him do it, once again conscious I might have to use my weapons on him, depending on how tonight went.

I kept that thought in the much quieter parts of my mind, however.

Black and I hadn't talked much when I got back to the restaurant, or while we geared up in that dark corner of parking lot under a broken streetlamp.

He'd looked me over in the restaurant when I slid back into the leather booth across from him, after leaving Ian. I'd seen his gold eyes narrow, even as his mouth twisted in a harder grimace.

"You smell like him," he said, wrinkling his nose. "He pissed all over you, didn't he? I'm not sure if I should be flattered or annoyed."

He said it like he was trying to sound amused, but I didn't see much real amusement on him. Truthfully, he'd sounded more angry than annoyed.

"Ian doesn't have to piss on me," I said, giving him a warning look as I picked up my glass of wine.

Black's frown deepened, but he didn't answer.

The rest of the time we mostly just sat there, eating and drinking.

Our conversation remained minimal through most of the meal, although he did answer a few questions I had about the action-packed evening he had planned.

Black finally seemed to make up his mind to ignore me altogether towards the end of the main course, pulling out his large-screened phone and using it for what looked like research. Watching him, I doubted he was getting most of his information from public sources.

I decided to ignore him as well.

We'd finished our food entirely by then and he'd ordered us both cappuccinos.

I turned on my phone, intending to scan articles on the wedding killer to see if there had been any new developments. Of course, I'd managed to forget over that span of however-many minutes that my phone had been switched off for hours.

It lit up like a Christmas tree the second I turned it on.

Six voice messages from Ian, which he'd already more or less warned me about. A dozen more texts, most of those ending in question marks, also from Ian.

He wasn't the big winner of the evening though.

I had another twenty or so texts from Nick, each employing caps-lock more liberally than the one before. The progression was pretty easy to follow.

1:19 PM - *Letting Black go. Lawyers here. Sorry about before.*

And then:

1:42 PM - *Hello? Did you leave your phone off again?*

And then:

2:04 PM - *Don't be pissed, Miri. Call me. I need to talk to you.*

And then:

2:22 PM - *Outside Black's. Downtown. CALL ME.*

I scrolled through a few more like that.

And then:

3:04 PM - *SICK? ARE YOU F-ING KIDDING ME? Even gomey didn't believe that horseshit. Call me.*

I scrolled through a few more.

4:25 PM - *SENT ANGEL BY YOUR HOUSE. NO ONE HOME. CALL ME. I MEAN IT.*

I scrolled through a few more threats, seemingly one every half-hour, then saw:

8:10 PM - *I'M PUTTING OUT A FUCKING APB AND*

CALLING IAN IF YOU DON'T ANSWER ME IN THE NEXT HOUR. NOT KIDDING.

Letting out a growling sigh of frustration, I ignored Black's questioning look as I tried to decide if I should answer. Nick would know from his phone settings that I'd finally seen his messages, assuming he was still watching.

Which he would be. Of course.

Taking a breath, I decided I didn't have much choice.

9:02 PM - *Chill the fuck out! Didn't have my phone. Went out for drinks with Lacey when my headache got better. Ian's back. We'll talk tomorrow.*

I didn't have to wait long for an answer.

9:03 PM - *BULLSHIT. WHERE ARE YOU, MIRI? I NEED TO TALK TO YOU. NOW.*

Grumbling under my breath again, I typed in a note.

That time I did the caps-lock thing too.

9:03 PM - *WELL YOU CAN'T. IAN'S BACK. TOMORROW NICK. I MEAN IT.*

I didn't wait for him to answer.

Turning off my phone, I flipped it over and pried the casing off the back with my fingers, remembering how Ian had traced me here using my SIM card. Once I had the casing off, I removed the SIM card itself. After pulling my wallet out of my purse, I stuck it in a pouch near the credit card slots.

I pulled out one of the other SIM cards I had in there then and checked the number.

I'd gotten in the habit of switching out SIM cards where it made sense, using my office phone and a forwarding service as my main number for business cards and the rest.

Truthfully, I picked up the habit watching Ian, who had four or five on him at any given time, given his job, along with some kind of high-tech security app that allowed him to change his actual IMEI number, which identified the phone itself, independently of the phone number, I mean. He probably thought I didn't notice how often he switched those out, but he didn't deny it when I remarked on it, either.

For me it was simply one more byproduct of working closely with the police and having a fiancé with an obscenely high security clearance.

Also, yeah, my work put me in contact with some dangerous people.

Given that, I switched out SIMs every few months usually. I only gave the direct line to close friends, and then only when they asked—usually they just used the forwarding service like everyone else, since most claimed it was a pain in the ass to reprogram my number as often as I changed it. I also had a second SIM card I used for work when I had a client I thought might be dangerous. I'd gotten in the habit of giving that number to Nick, too.

I carried a third one as well, that no one knew about but me. I used that one only for emergencies. I contemplated using it now.

"Don't bother," Black said. "If they're tracking you, they already know where you are. Unless you have the same program as your boyfriend."

I glanced up and found Black's eyes on me, more specifically on my hands.

"Okay with a different bar?" I asked, lifting an eyebrow.

Black didn't bother to nod.

While I popped the battery out of my phone with my fingers, he just lifted a hand to our waiter, signaling for the check.

About thirty or so minutes later we were in a different bar

on Clement Street. We'd taken a cab most of the way there, after walking down the hill towards Ocean Beach.

The second bar was darker, dingier and more of a hole in the wall, with blacklight posters on the walls and Asian pop music playing out of the retro-styled jukebox. Most of the patrons were Chinese hipster kids who probably worked at tech companies in the valley. The majority of them looked barely twenty-five to me, but somehow, they seemed even younger.

They ignored us, which suited me fine.

At the same time, we blended in weirdly, since most of them wore dark colors and had their eyes locked on their phones just like Black did.

I ended up doing the same.

I popped the battery back in my phone, knowing it was unlikely to ping off cell towers without the SIM card, and that I should be able to use the bar's wifi for basic surfing. Once we'd settled at a table near the back exit, I finally got a chance to scan for articles on the wedding murders myself, looking to see if there had been any new developments.

There hadn't been really.

I winced when I saw an image of Black being led into the police station in handcuffs, thinking immediately of Ian watching the nightly news. Black's head and face had been blurred though, so all you could see were the rings on his fingers under the cuffs and the black clothes and his arms and hands covered in blood. Reporters mentioned that the police let him go a little more than twenty-four hours later.

Nothing I saw, either in photo or video, showed Black's face.

They hadn't even mentioned his name.

Black must have damned good lawyers to keep that stuff out of the news, without even the obligatory "alleged" and "person of interest" words attached...much less off the dozens of voyeuristic and conspiracy sites that obsessed on the wedding murders online. Most of those sites had a pet conspiracy about the identity of the killer (or in some cases, killers), as well as a creative diversity in motives, connections to the victims and so on.

At the end of an hour of reading through posts, I still didn't feel like I'd learned much. Eventually I'd sighed, popped the battery out of the back of my phone, and wandered to the bar to order a caffeinated soda.

We left the bar right around ten-thirty.

Truthfully, the idea of us doing anything that night apart from getting arrested—or, best case, freezing our asses off waiting for someone who never bothered to show—seemed like an insane long-shot to me now.

Assuming Black wasn't the killer himself, of course.

Following his graceful and nearly-silent steps down a sand-and-dirt trail between pine and redwood trees heading north, I found myself thinking again how dangerous this was, even apart from the sheer improbability of our catching the killer.

Why the hell would I believe Black about any of this?

Even if I believed he didn't intend to kill me—which for some utterly irrational reason I still did—why would I believe his crazy theory about other-dimensional astrology systems and their connection to alien wedding rituals and anti-human terrorist plots?

While all of it sounded equally implausible in Black's penthouse that afternoon, strangely, it hadn't sounded as dangerous.

But now, the idea that we could just pop down here to check out Black's theory in the middle of the night without police back-up struck me as deeply delusional, and not only because Black was armed like he expected to be breaking into a maximum security penitentiary.

We were reaching the edge of the wooded park.

I could see a brighter glow of orange-tinted streetlights in the distance, even though we faced the back-end of the building, which remained in shadow. We'd just crossed a small wooden foot bridge when the path sloped up to the last line of trees. Beyond that was a landscaped lawn that wrapped around the structure up to the fountain and courtyard.

We were about to enter the park-like grounds when Black motioned for me to follow him to the left instead, taking me through a path-less cluster of trees around the west side of the building. Within a few minutes I saw the stone patio and tables outside the lower floor restaurant. Black used military hand-gestures to let me know we were entering the building there.

It hit me again that we were really breaking in. I found myself gripping the handle of the gun poking out by the left side of my ribs, but I didn't draw it.

I liked having him in front of me at least.

Well, assuming he wasn't working with anyone else.

Glancing behind me, I opened my mind, listening for the thoughts of other people.

People besides me and Black, that is.

When I did, Black came to a dead stop.

He looked back at me sharply, his irises picking up a faint light from...somewhere...some light behind me, maybe from something on the grounds of the military-owned land, or maybe the moon.

Before I could think about why he was looking at me like that, he took a long step in my direction. Catching hold of my arms in his fingers, he lowered his head, speaking softly in my ear once he was near enough.

"We're tracking one like me," he said. "And you."

"Yeah?" I said, just as quiet.

"Yeah? Don't do that," he said, lower still. "Don't try to read me. Don't look for them with your mind. They might feel it...or hear it."

Moving my head away from his, I could only stare up at him in the dark.

His expression didn't move.

"I don't want them to know what you are," he added, harder.

The silence between us deepened.

"You hearing me, doc?" he whispered. "You can't control that, I want you to head back. To the car. Now."

Weirdly, his words caused me to relax.

Which, if he'd been a psychopath, might have been their purpose.

I shoved that fleeting thought out of my mind.

"Got it," was all I said.

Like him, I avoided words with hard sibilant, or "s" sounds.

"Okay?" he said.

I nodded, my hand still on the gun. "I got it. Go."

He nodded, then turned, walking with those oddly silent steps of his through the trees. We didn't emerge out onto the lawn itself until the last possible minute, after we'd walked the tree-lined road with the golf course on our left and the museum on our right, bringing us directly across from that outdoor patio with its closed umbrellas over round tables.

I followed him out onto the lawn, conscious that I was holding my breath as we approached the patio. We walked between those stone tables and dark, folded umbrellas. I could see the streetlights to our left, at the front of the building. I could even see part of the view past the building itself, although the trees of the Presidio made most of that dark apart from shimmering reflections of the moon on occasional glimpses of water.

Within seconds, I found myself with Black against the white wall of the building. We stood just to the right of the glass doors leading into the restaurant's main dining area. I was about to ask Black how he planned to get us past the alarms and security cameras when he touched the headset he wore and spoke in a murmur.

"Dark," I heard him murmur.

I happened to be looking at the control box to the alarm over a doorway inside the restaurant. Being pitch black in there, it was the only light I could see beyond a faint illumination beyond the arch of that same door.

I watched the indicator light turn from red to green.

A bare second later, Black turned to me. "Ready?"

I nodded, my heart hammering in my chest. I was never someone who froze in combat situations. Still, I wasn't one of those weirdos who got off on them either.

"Liar," Black murmured next to me.

I wasn't sure which thing he meant, so I only frowned.

Giving me a faint smile, he inserted a metal cylinder into the locking mechanism under the metal handle of the door. I held my breath as he turned it easily to the right, hitting a faint resistance before there was an audible click.

A master key of some kind.

Withdrawing and pocketing the cylinder, Black pushed open the sliding glass door.

Then we were inside, walking between tables in the dark.

Both of us had guns in our hands now.

I was more conscious of the possibility of friendly fire than unfriendly at that point—meaning I didn't want to accidentally shoot some poor security guard who came down here looking for a snack.

I knew they must have actual living guards in a place like this.

When I'd brought that up to Black over dinner, he'd seemed unconcerned.

"Cameras will go down when my team pulls the plug on the alarms," he'd told me, leaning over his plate of half-eaten steak to show me some flickering of program code sent to him by his people.

"They're working on getting us video feed streaming to the monitors. It'll have to be a loop, so there's some chance it'll be picked up by their software...although my team is aiming for a loop of twenty minutes, so we likely have that, minimum, to get inside, unless they pick up on the signal tampering. Or notice the moon."

"The moon?" I'd paused with a forkful of grilled salmon halfway to my mouth. "What does that mean?"

"There's a moon tonight," he said, equally dismissive as he tapped the glass window with the backs of his fingers. "Twenty minutes is long enough for it to move. They'll take the sample loop as close as they can, but depending on cloud cover and the moon's position..."

"Okay," I said. "I got it."

I was staring out the window though, thinking, and Black must have seen it on my face. For some reason, he didn't ignore it that time.

"What?" he said.

"That spiral pattern," I said, looking away from the window. "You know what it is?"

He made a vague gesture with one hand. "I might."

"What is it?"

"I said 'might,'" he said, sharper, his sculpted lips turning in a faint frown. "That wasn't a figure of speech, doc." His expression still hard, he made a more conciliatory wave with the same hand, lowering his voice. "I've seen it before. Not only in this world. I haven't had time to research it fully, and I wasn't familiar with the group back in our home dimension...but the symbol's not dissimilar to something I remember there."

"Where?" I said.

"I just told you."

I shook my head. "No. I mean what was the context? Secular? Religious? Political? Where did you see it? In that...other place?"

"I saw it written on walls. And on flags belonging to a sect operating there. A religion, I guess you could say."

I frowned. "*Was* it a religion?"

"It would probably be most accurate to call it a radical sect of a religion," he said, taking a sip of his wine. "One with... political aspirations. The religion itself was more mainstream." Hesitating, he met my gaze. "It was race-related. The three spirals, they represented the three main races. That was a big part of their ideology."

"There were three races there? Three *humanoid* races?"

"Yes." Chewing on a piece of steak and swallowing, he shrugged. "Well...one was extinct. Or a myth. Depends on who you asked. Only two existed when I was there."

I nodded, deciding to shelve that for now, too.

Then, thinking about his words, I shook my head, putting down my fork.

169

"What exactly do you plan to do?" I said, wiping my hands on the napkin in my lap. "Shoot the guy? Talk to him?"

"Both, perhaps," he said, giving me a cryptic smile. His eyes grew more serious when he added, "I want to know *what* he is first, Miriam. And if he's working alone. If I didn't need to know those things, I'd just call the police. Let your friend Tanaka handle it."

I let out a disbelieving laugh. "Right."

"I would," he said, sounding a little offended. "Why wouldn't I?"

I had no idea how to answer that. So I didn't.

I had to hope he had some plan, though.

Something beyond "talk to the guy."

Glancing at my watch, I hoped like hell Ian was dead asleep by now, too.

As I thought it, Black peered his head out of the doorway between the restaurant's main dining room and the hallway leading into the downstairs exhibit halls. I knew the staircase to the upper floors lived near the restaurant's entrance as well. After Black checked to make sure the coast was clear, he turned to me. He showed me a screen with dark blue letters on a pitch black background, presumably to minimize brightness.

Virus has been activated, the letters read. *Security will be busy. 10 mins.*

He typed again, his fingers moving with a mechanical precision.

They'll check down here last, the letters read. *We need to hide before they do. My people will keep motion sensors off if they can. Can't count on it.*

I gestured my confusion.

He typed again. *Under the pyramid. Angel.*

170

That time I just nodded, tightening my hands on the gun.

I should have known.

Those spirals couldn't have been a coincidence.

Swallowing my misgivings, I followed Black, my gun pointed down but still in front of me. I kept my eyes on his back as he moved silently across the tile floor. I also kept my ears and eyes open, glancing up as we passed beneath the staircase, listening with my ears that time, even as I scanned the dimly lit passage with my eyes.

I remembered his warning about not trying to use my mind in here.

Suddenly, that felt like a pretty big handicap.

I looked down even as Black aimed us down a smaller corridor.

I remembered the passageway. Now that I knew where we were going, I tried to remember the exact layout of this lower floor. The near-perfect darkness didn't help, partly because everything looked so different than it had that afternoon, but also because it was easy to get turned around, forget what direction we were traveling. I had the blueprints memorized according to their relation to the directions of the compass, so losing that disoriented me.

Alcove lighting under a few works of art hanging in the hallway helped me to find my way back to the map, as well as dim, floor-level illumination around two doors we passed. I also saw one flickering, cracked Exit sign, and a few times, smaller panel lights, probably from security cameras that Black seemed to think were all switched off.

None of those lights traveled far.

Truthfully, they disoriented me as much as they helped in terms of seeing what was around us, breaking up my night vision if I looked at them too long. But they got me oriented more or less to the blueprints again.

Most of the floor was completely dark; I wasn't sure if that was Black's doing too, meaning something related to whatever his people had done to turn off security. Even the bathrooms we passed were dark, but maybe the security guards used a different set upstairs.

I still hadn't heard anyone.

We walked through another archway and into an exhibit room that was nearly pitch black. My heart pounding harder, I raised the gun, my fingers resting on the barrel just above the trigger. Indistinct shapes made me startle a few times, seeing what might have been people.

In all three cases, they turned out to be sculptures.

We left through another arched doorway on the other side and entered a room that appeared to be mostly furniture. If I was remembering accurately, this room was a historical re-creation of a European King's parlor room, someone from Bourbon France, I think. I remembered marveling over the details they'd included that afternoon: old musical instruments and sheet music and a writing desk along with gorgeous bookshelves filled with rare books, many of which appeared to be real, on loan from some collector or another.

This had to be one of the rooms with motion sensors, I thought.

Some of the items in here had to be priceless.

The realization didn't do much for my nerves. It was too quiet. I found myself wondering exactly what Black's people had done to keep the security guards so occupied upstairs.

When we reached the next archway, I knew something was wrong.

Light came from that entrance.

I'd expected *some* light under the pyramid itself, of course. Even with the partially cloudy sky, the moon was nearly full, so I'd expected there to be a blueish glow in the room housing the statue of the angel.

But the light I could see in the room ahead wasn't blue. It flickered and glowed a darker yellow, nearly orange where it leaked into the adjacent exhibit hall.

Like fire.

My heart hammered louder under my ribs, feeling like it might crack a bone. I was having trouble breathing, although I couldn't yet attach anything concrete to the feeling.

Still, some part of me knew...felt it...

Black came to a dead stop when he saw the same light.

Then he walked carefully around it, avoiding the illuminated swath of floor as he headed for the arched entryway connecting the two rooms. When he reached the shadowed segment of wall to the right, he went completely motionless, staring inside the room at an angle without letting any part of himself touch the light. Then he turned, his gold eyes strangely visible in the dark.

He motioned with a hand, again using military signals to tell me to walk to his left, to go around the light to the other side of the open archway, opposite him.

Lowering the gun, I did as he asked.

I stepped carefully, following the shadow all the way back to get to the other side of the arch without being seen by anyone in the lit room.

I reached the opposite side of the door seconds later. Remaining in shadow, I stared into the lit side of the room I could see without putting my face into the opening and therefore the light.

From here, that flicker of orange and yellow definitely looked like candlelight.

Fire, anyway.

I also saw a snippet of what looked like writing on the far wall. I didn't recognize any of the characters, but that wasn't what drew my attention at first. The symbols had been done in ragged, uneven brush strokes, using a dark red liquid. I really, really hoped that dark red "paint" wasn't what my mind immediately wanted to tell me it was.

I could smell it though, even from here.

That dense, coppery scent wafted in the air, seemingly made worse by the flickers of candlelight. I caught the faintest whiff of smoke too, but somehow it was that coppery smell my brain fixated on the most intently.

Maybe it was some animal instinct still hard-wired in my DNA.

I glanced at Black, and saw him lurking in the shadow as well, his gold eyes scanning the opposite segment of the exhibit hall. It occurred to me that from where he stood, Black had a much wider view of the overall room. I couldn't see the angel statue from where I was, just the edge of that writing on the wall covering part of one painting, along with the archway leading out what must be the southwest end of the central exhibit chamber.

From his angle, Black must be able to see the actual statue.

Even as I thought it, he frowned.

Then he let out an audible sigh—audible enough that I jumped, realizing only then how quiet both of us had been.

He looked at me, meeting my gaze with his lion-like eyes.

"We're too late, doc," he said.

He spoke softly, but not in a whisper.

Before I could react, he re-holstered his gun. I stared at

him, uncomprehending as he entered the exhibit hall without hesitation, his mouth set in a grim line as he walked out into the light and crossed the threshold. I stood there, still gripping my own gun in both hands, breathing harder as some part of my brain continued to grapple with his words.

Unlike him, I kept my gun out as I followed him. I held it in both hands, if aimed at the floor. In fact, I only reinforced my grip on the handle as I walked out into the light.

As soon as I turned the corner, I let out an involuntary gasp. I saw her first...before I saw the rest, I mean.

I stared at her for a few full seconds before I made sense of any other part of the scene...or what her awkward pose meant.

Her arms were spread up and out in that same curved loop over her head. Her head itself tilted backwards, a dark red slash showing where her throat had been cut.

She wore a wedding dress.

Her dress flowed out longer in back than the ones in pictures of the other murders I'd seen, with a built-in train. Instead of lying flat in the simulated pose mirrored by the other two, she'd been stretched into that pose with the help of the angel and horse statue, as well as what must be wire or thread. Whatever it was, it didn't show up immediately in the flickering candlelight.

Someone had lit upwards of thirty or so white candles, using them to surround the angel statue, and to illuminate the killer's display.

One of each of her forearms had been tied to one each of the angel's wings. Her hands had been positioned carefully, in a way that again suggested wire or string holding them in that perfect, delicate-fingered position like a ballerina's pose.

Her legs had been posed into the exact same position as the other victims' as well, with the difference being that this one was more or less vertical versus being displayed on her back. The left leg stretched straight, the toe pointed and most of the leg visible below the dress, which had been bunched up in front nearly to her waist. The right leg had been bent at the knee, the toe also pointed and apparently tied up with the same mechanism that kept the hands in place.

Whoever had cut her throat sawed into the flesh and muscle so deep they'd nearly severed her head from her body. Her head hung at that grotesque angle as a result, the yawning cut facing the skylight, the surrounding skin of her neck bone-white in contrast.

Someone had carved the three spiral symbol at the base of her throat. From the amount of blood soaking her chest, I suspected they'd carved it there, as well. The symbol at her throat covered most of her collarbone area, appearing almost black in the candlelight.

I stared at her, knowing she was dead.

Moreover, she'd been dead for some time.

No blood covered the floor beneath her. None ran from that slash on her neck.

A metal pail stood on the stone tile floor in front of her, weirdly innocuous-looking. It had been placed with obvious deliberation however, since it stood in perfect symmetry with the displayed body and the statue, forming a triangular point between the angel's wings.

I winced when I realized a lot of the coppery smell came from that pail.

Covering my mouth and nose with one hand, I looked away from her, fighting nausea, even as I kept the gun pointed roughly in her direction.

My eyes shifted to the wall.

I could see two lines of symbols now, covering the length of the room on that side.

I had no idea what they meant.

"It's writing," Black breathed.

I glanced at him, realizing only then that I'd forgotten he was there.

"What language?" I said, my voice less than a whisper.

He gave me a grim look, not answering. Then he spoke a language I'd never heard before. His words rang out with an alien melodiousness, mixed with rougher, more guttural sounds that were somehow even more foreign.

A ringing silence fell after he finished.

Then he spoke again, in the same clear voice. It wasn't until he got a few words in that I realized he was translating the words that time, speaking English.

"*And a great wail rose when the gods spoke,*" Black said. "*...For the door to that other place must need be lost, and those on the other side forgotten...*"

When he finished speaking, the silence deepened once more.

In it, all I heard was the faint hiss of guttering candle flames.

"What does it mean?" I finally whispered.

Black looked at me.

Something in his eyes made him appear lost deep in thought, his mind a million miles away. I watched that more distant look fade, right before his expression hardened, making him look dangerous.

"It means he knows about me," he said.

He closed the distance between us is two long strides.

I didn't flinch but felt myself tense, gripping the gun I held more tightly, still aiming it towards the floor and roughly in the direction of the dead girl. If Black noticed, it didn't slow him down. He walked right up to me, his gold eyes even more animal in the candles' flames.

"...He knows what I am. We need to get out of here. Now, Miriam."

He caught hold of my arm.

As he did, an explosion ripped through the skylight overhead, knocking both of us down.

TEN
BECOMING THE HUNTED

Y EARS RANG. I COULDN'T HEAR ANYTHING ELSE.

I found myself rolling on my back on a tile floor with chunks ripped out of it. Dazed, smoke and dust in my eyes, I fought to see past the falling debris as pain screamed in my leg. I struggled to get to my side, to get up. I wasn't thinking clearly enough to articulate in my mind what I intended next, but my body moved anyway, just like it had in combat.

I looked for Black and found him lying on his back near a few chunks of stone tile, his eyes closed. I didn't see anything but small cuts on him from the glass, what might have been burns on his arms and face...but he looked unconscious. My eyes darted to the fire burning in the middle of the room. The woman in the wedding dress looked like some kind of demon as she burned, her up-stretched arms blackening as the fire ate through the fabric of her dress.

The gauzy fabric flamed higher as I watched, even as the fire leapt to her long hair.

I could smell her flesh burning even through the floating dust.

I was glad I couldn't see her face.

I started to move, to crawl towards Black, gasping in pain from whatever happened to my leg...

Someone had ahold of my arm then, and was dragging me backwards.

I fought to breathe, then to extricate myself from whoever it was. My struggle didn't last long; the pain in my leg ripped through me as soon as I kicked out, making me scream until I ran out of air.

I nearly blacked out the first time.

Whoever dragged me only tightened their grip. When my mind righted itself, I let out a cry, coughing in dust particles as I stared up at the hole in the ceiling where the skylight had been. Blackened at the edges, it belched smoke upwards in a high column through the opening.

But my view of the exhibit hall was disappearing. I grunted, crying out again as I got pulled over chunks of glass and ripped up stone tile, what felt like pieces of metal.

Coughing harder, I fought to free my arm of those steel-like fingers a second time and the person holding me squeezed the muscle and bone hard...so hard my mind blanked. When I opened my eyes next, they'd already dragged me into the darkness of a second exhibit room.

It wasn't Black...

I twisted my head and neck around to look at who pulled me along the slick floor, trying to see their outline in the dark. I couldn't see his face, or even get a clear idea of his size now that we were in full shadow.

Gloved fingers gripped my arm. I saw a glint of a watch,

silver like Black's military watch, but that glimpse definitely wasn't of the arm I remembered.

My mind woke up more, penetrating the shock and pain.

Black had been on the floor. Unconscious.

Whoever dragged me now, it couldn't be him.

"Let go," I managed, my voice hoarse and muffled in my own ears. "Stop. Please...I can walk...I can walk on my own now..."

Whoever it was didn't answer.

Maybe he didn't hear me.

I reached for my left side, looking for the handle of the gun I'd worn. I remembered I'd been holding it when the bomb went off. I must have dropped it. I reached for the right-side holster, but that one was empty too. So was the one lower down, at my hip.

"Hey!" I choked. "Hey...we have friends coming. Police..."

He yanked on me harder, and I felt...

Anger. A hell of a lot of anger.

So much it overwhelmed me briefly, blanking my mind.

It wasn't my anger.

But that bothered me less than the second realization I had.

Whoever held me, I didn't recognize their mind.

Moreover, they appeared to be shielding. They shielded like Black did when I tried to read him at the Cliff House restaurant. The emotions I felt came from a distance, a bare hint whispering through the cracks. I wouldn't have felt it at all, but for the sheer intensity of what lived the other side of that wall.

I twisted in his iron grip, biting my tongue against the blinding pain that spiked in my thigh when I moved. I craned my head and neck again, trying to see him, but he wore something on his face and head, in addition to covering his body and hands.

We came out of the next hallway and I saw his outline for the first time—definitely a man from his basic build and height.

Definitely *not* Quentin Black.

He wasn't tall enough. He wasn't big enough. He moved wrong.

I'd known that, of course. I'd known it before we left that burning room. Even so, something about seeing this alien shape, dressed all in black and wearing gloves, woke me up for real, for the first time since the bomb went off.

I let out a drawn-out shriek. It might have been a scream, if my lungs hadn't been so full of smoke and particulates from the caved-in ceiling in the other room. As it was, I choked out the sound, half a cough and half a broken, panicked yell.

Images of murdered women flickered behind my eyes.

The woman on the stainless steel slab. The one hanging from the bronze wings of that statue, burning, her arms outstretched, that cut in her throat like a silent scream. I fought to push away Zoe's face, which wanted to superimpose on the two girls.

Even though my right leg was the one I'd hurt, I yanked it up to my free hand, letting out a groan without letting the pain slow me down. Once I did, I saw it: a thick shard of glass stuck in the muscle of my thigh, right above my knee.

I didn't think. I didn't let myself think, or question whether what I intended to do was particularly wise.

Adrenaline slammed through my body, making my hand shake as I yanked the shard from my leg. The pain was immediate, blinding—it caused my whole body to jerk. I couldn't make a sound but somehow, I didn't pass out, or begin my slide back into full-blown shock. I didn't wait for the man dragging me to figure out what I'd done.

Twisting my head and neck, I only looked back long enough

to see exactly where he was. Then I swung the glass shard as hard as I could, sawing the jagged edge into the skin and flesh of the arm holding me.

A line of dark red swiftly opened above those black gloves.

Whoever held me let out a hissing gasp.

Right before they opened their fingers.

I felt heavily to the tile.

I didn't wait, but rolled to one side, letting out a cry as my weight came to rest on my gashed leg. I jerked myself up seconds later, using the wall and my good leg and a major dose of adrenaline. I regained verticality with a heavy gasp, then struggled to keep it.

Facing him, I hopped on one leg, using the wall for balance, still brandishing the jagged shard of glass.

I tried not to think about the fact that I might be bleeding out where I stood.

The man in front of me wore a black mask. Not a ski mask... something else.

Whatever it was, it covered everything but his eyes. The material looked hard, like plastic or metal. It gave him a creepy, dead-faced look, like a blank, expressionless doll. It also completely changed the shape of his face, making him impossible to identify.

He didn't even look human.

He turned his head slightly as I thought it. A small console light from the security box in the corridor glinted on the surface of the mask.

Metal. It had to be metal, just by how the light bounced off the burnished surface.

He just stood there, watching me.

I could almost feel him thinking, but I didn't try to determine that for sure, remembering what Black said about not letting him know what I was.

His eyes were light-colored through the holes in the mask, ghostly.

They were so light, in fact, I found myself thinking they had to be contacts — they looked almost white, or even colorless, like crystal. Then I remembered Black's weird-colored eyes and wondered if that was something to do with what he was.

Maybe all of Black's "people" had eyes like that.

The idea that this...person...might be like Black, brought my fear back in a rush.

It also caused me to take a step backwards.

He moved when I moved, holding the cut on his arm as he maneuvered closer, mirroring my steps. He halted when I brandished the piece of glass. Pressing my back to the wall, I looked around, breathing hard as I tried to decide what to do.

His knees bent slightly, lowering his body into a predatory crouch. I found myself flashing to a cat readying to spring, its tail lashing back and forth as it waited for its prey to flinch or look away.

I didn't take my eyes off him as I began to shuffle-walk sideways, sliding along the wall with my back and holding the glass shard higher. As I positioned my back to get me closer to the stairs, he held up a hand, almost a peace gesture.

Again, something in the gesture reminded me of the strange way Black moved.

My other hand pressed against the cut in my thigh. After the barest pause at his gesture, I continued to make my way along the wall, thinking if I could just get to the staircase...

The man raised his other hand.

That time, he gripped a gun. Maybe even my gun.

He aimed it at my chest.

That glimmer of hope I'd been grasping faded.

Fear fought to wipe out the remainder of my thoughts.

Black was in the other room. Lying on the floor. Maybe burning by now. I'd never seen him move after that blast. If he'd woken up, he would have come after me, wouldn't he? He wouldn't have just let this psycho just take me.

But I never saw him move. Never heard him make a sound.

Had he been...could he have really been...

My mind stuttered around the word.

Black couldn't be—

"Dead?" the man in front of me said.

His voice made me jump.

Partly for the volume—he didn't whisper but spoke loudly, above the sound of the fire. It was the first speech I'd heard above a murmur since we'd left Clement Street.

But mainly, it was his voice itself.

The word came out machine-like, distorted. His voice sounded cartoonishly deep, with a discernible echo. He had a voice-scrambler built into the mask, my mind told me a half-second later. That wasn't a real voice. I was still moving gradually along the wall as I thought it, shifting my feet and weight instinctively.

I halted when he clicked off the gun's safety, renewing his grip on the handle before he aimed it back at my chest.

Still staring at me, he raised his other hand. With a strange precision, he wagged his index finger at me. Somehow, it was that weirdly archaic gesture that got my mind moving again.

"Stay," he said, as if speaking to a dog.

As before, the word distorted, deep and mechanical-sounding through the scrambler.

I clenched my jaw, thinking again about Black.

He wasn't dead. He couldn't be dead.

The man in front of me laughed. The laughter was even more eerie through the voice box. It sounded like the laughter of a super-villain.

"I think *abandoned you* is more likely," he said. He paused, as if waiting for a reaction from me. When I didn't move, or answer, he spoke again through the mechanical scrambler, and I heard humor in his voice. "From what I hear, Mr. Black never was all that reliable when it comes to females. Not that I blame him for that..."

Biting my lip, I fought to think.

Where are the guards? my mind wondered.

Where were the fire alarms? The sprinklers? Had Black's people turned off all of that, too? Or had the masked man disabled everything prior to setting off the bomb?

"I dress you up," he said in that stilted, mechanical voice. "You all look so pretty, dressed up. I can forget what you are. I can forget...everything. Everything."

I didn't answer, still fighting to think. Did he want an audience? Should I be trying to get him to engage, keep him talking to me? Even through the scrambler I could hear emotion in his voice, some flicker of passion. He was angry. He felt powerless maybe. Frustrated. My mind fuzzed. I couldn't make it work well enough to decide what to say.

My leg throbbed. I was getting light-headed. I'd lost too much blood.

"We will bring balance to this world," the man said in his metallic voice. "Just like we did the other one. We will be legion here...it will be like it was in the beginning again. Pure." His voice grew harder, audibly angry even through the scrambler. "There

186

must be...sacrifices. There must always be sacrifices along the way..."

"Sacrifices?" I said. "Is that what those girls are? Sacrifices?"

He only stared at me through the metal mask.

"How?" My voice shook. "How will you do it? Bring balance to the world?"

He didn't answer that either.

I could still hear the flames rising and sparking and spreading in the other exhibit rooms. The fire seemed to be sucking oxygen out of my lungs where I stood. The smoke was getting denser as well, harder to see through. I remembered all of the paintings, the priceless furniture. The noise of the fire seemed to get louder as I thought it. Then another sound rose at the bare edges of my hearing.

I listened, thinking I was imagining it...

But the sound grew louder.

Sirens. Distant, but definitely coming this way.

Even as I thought it, there was a popping sound above us, in the ceiling.

I flinched violently, looking up...

The sprinklers turned on, spraying water down on our heads.

In that bare instant of me looking up, the man in the metal mask lunged at me. He slammed into me with an arm and fist, knocking my hand holding the shard of glass. The sudden, precise blow forced me to let go.

Before my mind caught up, the glass had already left my fingers.

Stepping back, he kicked me right where the shard had been embedded in my leg. He did that with equal precision, hitting hard and down with the heel of his boot.

My injured leg crumpled.

I fell with zero resistance. My knees and palms slammed into the tile floor and I let out a hard gasp, choking on the scream that rose to my throat. It felt like the bones in my forearms splintered from the impact.

Looking up, I blinked against the onslaught of water, fighting to see.

The man in front of me raised the gun, aiming it at my face.

I let out a gasp, closing my eyes, bracing myself.

He wasn't going to wait.

No ritual for me. No spiral carvings in my chest while I screamed in pain.

I was just dead.

But the pause stretched. The gun didn't go off.

As I crouched there, panting, it crossed my mind to wonder why he'd dragged me out here in the first place. Why not just let me burn, like Black? Why not shoot me where he found me? I matched his victim profile, but I strongly suspected I wouldn't be getting the white dress or the caked on make-up, either. None of it made any sense...but I couldn't read him at all, even though I was actively trying now, which reminded me of something else.

Whoever this guy was, Black had been right.

The man in the metal mask was definitely like him.

Zero advantage, Miriam. I guess that whole psychic thing had been more of a survival crutch in wartime than I'd realized.

The man above me let out another of those grim chuckles. Even though he'd done it once before, the sound of it through the metallic-sounding scrambler made me wince.

"You were never meant to exist at all," he said. His voice sounded colder, even through the scrambler. "You are a disgusting, filthy abomination...an animal..."

188

I stared up at him through the falling water, confused.

Did he mean humans? People not like him and Black?

Or me, specifically?

Still staring at him, I felt my confusion worsen. What was he waiting for? Why hadn't he shot me? I could almost feel his indecision as he stood over me.

I closed my eyes, gasping for air through the water running down my face and into my mouth. Tensing for the gunshot I still expected, I nearly jumped out of my skin when another voice ripped through the quiet, one I definitely recognized.

"Police!" Nick Tanaka yelled, even as lights clicked on around us, showing at least ten guns on us from the staircase. "Put it down! Now!"

Relief exploded through me, so much it nearly brought tears to my eyes.

I looked to my left from where I knelt on the floor in the water from the sprinklers. I immediately saw Nick in front of about six other plainclothes officers, a light pressed against the barrel of his gun. I saw fury in his expression, so intense that I barely recognized his face, even apart from the dim light.

That fury wasn't trained at me though.

I couldn't even be certain he'd recognized me at that point. Rather he stared at the masked man standing over me, looking like he was having to restrain himself from shooting him on the spot. It hit me suddenly that Nick thought the man in the mask was Quentin Black.

Somehow, the realization almost made me laugh.

Then I remembered Black himself.

"In the other room!" I called out, pointing towards the opening into the exhibit hall. "Man down...in the other room! Call an ambulance!"

Nick barely gave me a glance, his focus still on the gunman.

"Put it down," Nick said, his voice a growl. "You have two seconds. Or we'll put you down like a rabid dog..."

Looking away from Nick's face, I stared back at the gunman. He hadn't moved. I didn't feel any fear on him.

When I looked up at his face, I didn't see any fear in those crystal-colored eyes, either.

If anything, the glimmer of feeling I got off him felt closest to humor.

"It's sweet, how you worry about him," he said through the voice scrambler. "I'll be sure and let him know...when I run into him next."

"Who are you?" I said, still fighting to focus through the falling water.

I swear I saw the visible flesh around his eyes crinkle in what had to be a smile.

Before I could speak, he flipped the gun in his hand, so fast I couldn't track the motion. Before I could blink, he swung his arm. The black handle of the gun rose into my vision.

Then it slammed into my temple, making my vision flash white.

...Right before everything went dark.

ELEVEN
THE OTHER SIDE OF THE TABLE

I SAT AT A GUNMETAL GRAY TABLE, UNDER BRIGHT-SEEMING LIGHTS.
My body curled around the metal chair, hitting every uncomfortable dent and bump that made up the seat and back. The chair had been bolted into the floor within a few feet of the table...close enough that I could rest my cuffed wrists on the scratched surface.

It was the opposite side of that same table from where I'd been sitting only days before.

This time, it was me wearing handcuffs.

Unlike Black, I wasn't chained to the floor, however. They'd left my ankles free.

Instead of someone like me sitting across the table, I found myself looking at Nick and Angel, the latter of whom looked uncomfortable and angry and borderline confused, although I couldn't tell at what exactly.

Either way, she refused to sit but instead stood by the one-way mirror set in the wall across from me, watching me with that confusion and anger and discomfort, almost like she didn't know me at all, or doubted whether she did. I honestly couldn't tell if she was angry at me or Nick at that point though...or just the situation more generally.

"So you're saying it wasn't Black who had the gun on you?" Nick said.

It had to be the twentieth time he'd asked me that question.

He'd started before I even got out of the hospital.

I was familiar with the repetition game, of course. I'd watched Nick do it to plenty of other perps. I'd seen him do it in Afghanistan, too.

I was also familiar with the whole "informal interview" request to try and get something out a potential suspect before they lawyered up. Truthfully, if I'd had a real lawyer of my own, meaning someone whose card or phone number I had on hand, I probably wouldn't have agreed to the interview at all, but as it was, I knew a public defender wouldn't help me much and I hadn't been able to get ahold of Ian when I used my one phone call.

So basically, I was killing time until Ian got my message and sent in the cavalry.

Assuming he still wanted to, that is...which might depend on if Nick had spoken to him already too, and what he might have told him.

So yeah, I wasn't totally blind to what Nick was doing.

He didn't have anything concrete on me yet, or they would have processed me for real and read me my rights.

I also knew the strategy behind his asking me the same thing over and over again, *ad nauseum*...but I wasn't sure if he was even consciously employing that strategy yet.

Truthfully, it sounded mostly like he was just angry.

Either his acting chops had gotten a lot better in the last week or so, or he really was stuck in a kind of mental loop around me and Black. That same part of him seemed convinced that if he asked me the same question enough times, he might eventually get me to not only speak, but to give him the answer he wanted.

Or maybe just the answer he believed had to be true.

I was really tired of playing though.

"You know it wasn't him," I said, glaring at Nick before I looked at Angel, who avoided my stare, folding her muscular arms and leaning against the wall by the one-way window. "You *know* it wasn't. You have to know that...you were there."

Nick scowled, leaning over the table. "I know we can't pin it on him, Miri. Not yet. Not without you. That's not exactly the same thing."

"So you don't care if you actually catch the guy who set off the bomb...or who tried to kill me?" I didn't flinch when he aimed a hard stare at me, and my voice stayed equally cold. "You just want to bring Black in for...what? Your dick issues? Your pride? Fuck the truth. Is that the kind of cop you are now, Nick?"

His eyes turned a considerably darker shade of brown.

"We know he was there, Miri," he said through gritted teeth. "We *know* he was involved."

"How?" I demanded. "How do you know that?"

"You mean apart from the fact that you practically told us as much? You said 'man down,' Miri. You said it...I fucking *heard* you!"

"So?" I said, throwing up my hands as much as I could in the cuffs. "Even if that were true...that would more or less point to the gunman *not* being Black, wouldn't it?"

"What was he doing there, Miriam?" Nick snapped. "What were *you* doing there?"

I shook my head, staring down at the surface of the table.

Exhaling in frustration, I combed my fingers through my hair.

"You didn't find anyone in that other exhibit hall. Did you, Nick?" I said.

But Nick went on as if I hadn't spoken.

"...It would speed things up considerably if you would at least testify that you went there of your own volition. That Black went there with you. That you broke into the Legion of Honor together." He clenched his jaw, hard enough to make the muscle in his cheek jut out. "Of course, it would help even more if you told us *why,* Miri. If you gave me some clue what the fuck you were doing there? What you meant to accomplish?"

"Don't you have him in custody?" I said, leaning over the table towards Nick. "The man who tried to kill me...don't you have him?" When I got nothing but silence from the two of them, I bit my lip, glancing at Angel before I looked back at Nick. "How could he have *possibly* gotten away? There was no way out of that lower structure...none. He set off a fucking bomb, Nick. You had like twenty officers there. Are you really saying—"

"You saw him do that?" Nick shot back. "You saw your so-called 'masked man' set off the bomb in the courtyard?"

"Do you have him in custody or not, Nick?" I demanded.

No one had given me a real answer on that, either.

Maybe, like Nick, some part of me wanted to keep asking it until they told me what the hell happened. I still had gotten almost zero information about what transpired between the time that masked man hit me in the head with the butt of my own gun and when I woke up in the hospital, gasping in pain as a nurse cleaned and disinfected my leg.

Not long after that, an intern had come in to stitch up the cut and bandage it.

The end product still throbbed dully, even after I washed down a few Vicodin. Moreover, I felt strangely vulnerable because of the injury, and maybe from being high on the painkillers now, too. I was also so tired it took work to make coherent sentences.

The bandage itself made a bulky lump on my leg, large enough that I now wore men's dark blue sweat pants, given to me by Angel out of the police locker room's lost and found. All they'd had at the hospital were scrubs, so Nick had Angel bring them for me, presumably so he could drag me down to the station.

Still, I guess I could blame myself for that, too. After all, I'd given them permission to move me from the hospital.

Stupid me, I'd thought I was actually going to be sent home.

One more reason being high on drugs right then made me nervous.

I knew Nick was taking advantage of that fact, which angered me, too.

"I need a lawyer," I said, rubbing my face. "I can't do this right now, Nick."

"Just a few more questions."

"Not until you answer some of mine," I snapped, dropping my hands and looking up at him. "How did he get away, Nick? How is that even possible?"

He and Angel looked at one another.

I bit my lip, fighting harder than maybe I ever had in my life to keep my promise to myself not to use my psychic abilities on either of my friends.

I already knew I might have to break that promise, given the current situation. That is, if I was going to get out of this without doing prison time. Wincing at the thought, I felt my heart beat harder as something else occurred to me.

"Where's Ian?" I said. "Is he here? Are you keeping him from me?"

The silence deepened.

In it, Angel and Nick again exchanged looks.

Then Nick gave me an incredulous stare. "Ian's in Bangkok, Miri."

"What?" I stared at him. Then, biting my lip, I shook my head. "No, Nick. He's not. I told you that already. Hell, *he* told you that...or I think he did..."

I trailed, my frown deepening.

Remembering Ian's words to me earlier that night—or really, the day before, since it had to be well into Thursday by now—I fought to think through the haze of painkillers.

Combing my fingers through my hair, I winced at knots and tangles, smelling smoke on my fingers once I'd finished. I looked between them.

Finally, I just shook my head. "Ian's back. I told you that. He's been back for hours...at least twelve by now. I thought you talked to him?"

Nick continued to stare at me, his expression suggesting he thought maybe I was in shock, or suffering from some other kind of mental breakdown.

"I did speak to him. In Bangkok. It's a twenty hour flight, Miri. Minimum."

"Didn't he tell you he was getting on a plane?" I said, ignoring his blank stare. "He told you he was coming back early, right? I saw him last night...at the Cliff House."

At their silence, I looked between the two of them again.

"Miri," Nick said, shaking his head. "You need to walk us through this. From the beginning."

"No," I said. "I don't. I need to talk to a lawyer, Nick. And you know it. Which means I probably need to talk to Ian...before I talk to you. So if he's here—"

"Miri, he's not in the fucking country!"

"The hell he isn't! I saw him tonight..." At Nick's stare, I corrected my words. "...Last night. I saw him last night. At the Cliff House. Like I said."

Again, Nick and Angel exchanged looks. That time, Angel shrugged. I could tell from the look on her face that she thought I'd cracked too.

My mind fought through the haze of Vicodin.

"What did you talk to him about?" I said. Looking up, I met Nick's gaze, realizing only then I hadn't included him in my entire thought process. "Ian," I clarified. "What did you tell him, when you talked? Did you tell him about Black?"

"Did I tell him about Black?" Nick leaned back, placing his hands on the metal table as his eyebrows rose. "Jesus, Miri. Why the hell do you think I called him? Of course I told him about Black. I felt like shit about it, actually...it scared the hell out of him."

"But did you tell him *about* him, Nick?" I said, my voice more insistent. "Did you tell him his name? Anything about who he was?"

"Of course I did! I wanted Ian to run a background check on the asshole. I gave him everything I had, Miri. Mug shots. Claimed name and address. Everything we got on his P.I. shop. The small amount I got on his military record. Fingerprints—"

"And when was that?" I cut in. "*When* did you talk to him, Nick? The first time?"

Again, Nick glanced at Angel.

Angel didn't return his look that time. Instead she continued to stare at me, her lips pursed as she seemed to be trying to read behind my expression. Unable to get her attention silently, Nick turned his focus back on me.

"This is important right now...why?" he said.

I swallowed, fighting to think through everything he'd just told me.

Ian. Ian knew who Black was when he met him.

He'd lied to me.

Suddenly, I felt a lot less confident that Ian was going to walk through that door. I also felt a lot less confident that I'd have a lawyer to look out for me anytime soon.

I was on my own.

My mind tilted, flashing me back to being inside a police station not unlike this one, describing to a different detective — an older African-American man with kind eyes, gray, tightly-cropped hair and a patient voice — what I knew about my sister's personal life.

That had been the night I came home and found police waiting for me.

The night I found out my sister had been killed.

"I don't think I'm going to answer any more questions," I said, looking up from where I'd been staring at my hands splayed on the metal table. It didn't really occur to me until I looked away that I'd been focused on my engagement ring, staring at it without seeing it. "This interview is over. Not another word until I speak to a lawyer."

"Miri," Nick began, frustrated.

I looked up, meeting his gaze. "I mean it, Nick. No more."

I wasn't even angry. I'd just...shut off.

"Miri," Nick began, his voice holding more concern that time. "Miri, be reasonable. I'm pissed off at you, yes. But I *do* see you as a victim in this. I think Black dragged you into this somehow, and I want to know why. I want to know how you know him, what you feel you owe him...whatever it is that he's got over you. It's not you we're after, Miri. I want Black. Do you understand? I'm trying to help you — "

He didn't get any further though.

The door opened with a bang.

Jumping, I turned, startled but already feeling a flush of relief.

Nick wouldn't interrupt an interview in process, so that meant someone else had done it. In the few seconds before my mind wrapped around the person standing there, I was sure it was Ian, that he'd come for me after all.

But the face of the woman standing there wasn't one I knew.

She exuded competence, however...and confidence. African-American, perfectly coiffed and maybe in her mid-forties, she carried a dark brown leather briefcase in both hands, had a fit, athletic body clad in a charcoal designer suit, and looked at me with an utterly clinical expression on her face. Her shoes looked Italian. Her hair had been sleeked back in a perfect bun. She wore light make-up and dark brown lipstick.

She couldn't have screamed "lawyer" more if she'd been wearing a sandwich board proclaiming herself as such.

Before she even opened her mouth, I knew Ian hadn't sent her.

I don't know how I knew, I just did.

"Ms. Fox?" she said to me, her voice melodic, perfectly professional.

I glanced at Nick, then back at her. "Yes?" I said.

She held out a hand, smiling at me. "I'm Victoria White. I'm your lawyer."

"My lawyer?" I glanced at Nick again, and from the scowl on

his face, I could tell he recognized the women from somewhere. I was about to turn, to speak to her again, when the door opened behind her.

That time, I recognized the man who walked in the room.

Bad toupee and all.

"Farraday," I murmured.

I looked at Nick, whose scowl had just deepened even more. Now at least I knew why. I felt my heart stutter briefly in my chest as I tried to make sense of the information standing in front of me, putting the pieces together even as I doubted the obvious conclusion.

Then another person entered the room.

He also, wore a suit.

I almost didn't recognize him, maybe for that reason alone. Then I looked at his face, and those gold eyes bored into mine, holding so much feeling that I flinched.

It was Quentin Black.

And he looked furious as hell.

HE FINISHED LOOKING AT ME, HIS EYES SHOWING A FLICKER OF RELIEF after they'd slid down me, as if he'd been unsure if I was even alive. I found myself looking at him, too, noticing the bruise on the side of his face, abrasions on his neck and forehead, along with a smattering of smaller cuts that must be from the glass raining down on us from that skylight. He looked more or less intact though, and a profound relief at discovering him not dead washed through me, nearly bringing tears to my eyes.

I blamed the Vicodin for that, too.

A faint smile touched his lips, almost like he heard me.

Then he turned his head, glowering at Nick with an anger I could actually *feel*, even from a few yards away.

"You're letting her go," he said, his voice an open threat. "Now, Tanaka."

Nick glared at him like he was the antichrist. "The hell I am. I should arrest you right now."

"On what charges?" Black shot back, even as Farraday held up a hand, as if to warn him to remain silent.

"How about blowing up a museum, for one?" Nick snapped.

Black let out a derisive snort.

Nick's eyes narrowed. "You want to tell us how you injured yourself in the last twenty-four hours, Mr. Black?" he said, staring pointedly at Black's bruised and cut hands.

Black looked about to speak, but that time, Farraday and his bad toupee stepped between the two of them, gripping his own briefcase even as he put up his other hand in a stop gesture aimed at Nick. The woman who'd introduced herself as Victoria White also moved deeper into the room, standing right next to me, in an unmistakably protective gesture.

"Do you intend to charge my client with something?" Farraday demanded.

Nick let out a disbelieving laugh, glaring at me. That time, the look in his eyes verged on disbelief, mixed with a betrayal that stood out on the surface.

"Which one?" he said coldly.

Victoria White set her briefcase down on the table next to me, now practically looming over where I sat. "Personally, I would primarily like to hear any charges you have against Ms. Fox, Inspector Tanaka. Although I do confess to some interest around any related charges levied against Mr. Black, assuming we should be taking your posturing towards him seriously right now." Her voice was clipped, but polite. "To answer your question, however, Ms. Fox is my client, technically speaking, as Mr. Black has retained me to look out for her well-being specifically. Therefore, I can only assume Mr. Farraday meant Mr. Black."

Nick glared at her, his expression openly hostile.

That time, it was Angel who intervened.

Stepping away from her position by the wall, she approached the group now clustered between me and the door. She held up a hand too, right before she addressed Victoria White.

"She's a witness to a possible terrorism case," Angel said, enunciating slowly, as if explaining something to someone incredibly slow-witted. "You can't possibly be questioning our motives in taking a statement from her?" Angel's voice grew a touch more bite. "...Or think we'll be the only ones to want to talk to her?"

"Not your motives, perhaps," Victoria White said, her eyes holding a denser meaning. "But your right? Most certainly."

Angel's lips pursed.

Victoria White didn't give her a chance to speak.

"...I would like a list of any agencies wishing to speak to my client, as well as the reasons. Before that, I insist on information relating to any charges filed by your department."

Angel let out a disbelieving laugh. "How about Homeland Security for one? The F.B.I.? How about—"

"I would like those requests in writing."

Victoria White's expression didn't waver, but her voice hardened audibly.

"...A list of agencies wishing to speak to my client, as well

202

as reasons and any charges filed is a bare minimum requirement for me to discuss when and if you may continue to speak to my client. You certainly can no longer do so when she's under the influence of heavy narcotics and probably in shock from a near-death encounter with a suspected serial killer..."

Her voice verged on openly angry when she added,

"Without sufficient cause and/or charges filed, I insist that you allow my client to come in for interviews *after* she's had a chance to recover from this harrowing ordeal. Preferably after she's been seen by at least one mental health professional and counseled around the obvious emotional distress this must have caused her..."

Her voice grew lower, even as she placed her hands on the table.

"I would also caution you to take *extreme care* in terms of charging my client at this time, detectives...before your department has definitively ascertained her exact role in this tragedy. If I were you, and I valued my job, I would make sure that the evidence was pretty damned close to unassailable in this case. After all, Ms. Fox fits the exact profile for the murder victims of this alleged serial killer..."

The silence deepened.

I saw Angel look at Nick. That time, even on drugs and despite their expressionless faces, I found myself understanding the glance that passed between them.

"Do you have any evidence of wrongdoing by my client?" Victoria White's voice still held that harder edge.

I glanced at Farraday, who was smirking at Nick, and then at Black, who was watching Nick with an openly furious expression on his face.

"You mean apart from finding her wearing body armor in

the middle of a break-in at the site of a bomb attack?" Nick said, returning Black's look with a murderous glare of his own.

"My client was found with absolutely no weapons on her person."

"She was wearing holsters," Angel said, her voice incredulous.

"...Which are not weapons," Victoria White returned at once. She waited a beat. "Am I to understand you're charging my client? If so, I would like to know what she is being charged with...and on what grounds? Again, tread lightly here, detectives...my firm is quite comfortable pursuing a civil suit if we feel any impropriety occurred that resulted in the unfair targeting of my client...particularly given our feeling that she is *very much* the victim here."

Another silence fell.

Glancing around at faces, I had a sudden, wholly inappropriate desire to laugh. I wanted to blame the Vicodin for this sudden flush of humor, but I found myself envisioning a tumbleweed blowing through the middle of the room, like a standoff at the OK Corral.

I looked at Black. That time, I found his eyes fixed on me.

I couldn't help noticing he looked pretty damned good in a suit, too.

The suit was black, of course, and had to be tailored to fit him that well, given his height and how broad his shoulders were. He wore a dark blue shirt under the mandarin collar jacket and no tie. I found myself looking him over for too long – again, I blamed the Vicodin – before I felt him noticing my stare and looked away.

When I did, I caught Nick's furious scowl at me and realized he'd watched me look at Black, too.

"When did you last talk to Ian?" I asked him compulsively.

Victoria White touched my arm, gently but insistently. "Please don't speak right now, Ms. Fox. They are going to do this right...or they're not doing it at all."

When I looked back towards Nick, I could already see on his face what was going to happen here. Whatever circumstantial evidence they had on me, they weren't going to risk holding me for it, not even with Homeland Security breathing down their necks.

"She's free to go of course," Nick said, still staring at me as he said it. His eyes glided up, taking in Victoria White. "We'd only hoped for her help at this point...you know, to catch a killer." He shifted the direction of his glare, aiming it at Black. "...One we know will kill again. Probably soon, unless we stop them. One who targets women like Ms. Fox, as you yourself pointed out. I'm sure you can understand our urgency in this."

"Of course," Victoria White said crisply.

She managed to convey pure professionalism and utter disdain in the same breath.

"But *our* main concern is for the well-being of our client, detective," she said. "Which I'm sure you can understand as well. So unless you are charging her this morning...I am taking her out of here. You can arrange times for interviews for her through my office."

She deliberately placed a pristine white business card on the table. The raised black letters faced Nick as she slid it towards him with two fingers.

Then she laid a hand on my shoulder.

Once more, her touch exuded protectiveness.

I knew it was her job to seem to be on my side, whatever her personal feelings. Even so, I found myself relaxing into the protective shield I felt from her that time. As I did, I realized again how exhausted I was, and then I was fighting a flush of gratitude so intense that it nearly brought tears to my eyes.

"We're leaving, Ms. Fox," she murmured to me gently, squeezing my shoulder. She looked at Nick. "Handcuffs, Mr. Tanaka?"

I just sat there, stunned, as Nick leaned over the table.

He didn't look at me as he used his key to unlock the handcuffs on my wrists.

Once he'd finished and the cuffs disappeared into one of his pockets, I just rubbed my wrists, not moving from the chair.

Then it hit me again that Nick and Angel really weren't going to try and stop me.

I rose shakily to my feet. Somehow, in all of that back and forth, I'd forgotten about my hurt leg. It crumpled under me as soon as I put weight on it, and I reached out, grabbing hold of the back of my chair and the table to catch my fall. Before my weight rested on either of my hands fully, Black was behind me, gripping my arms in both of his hands.

He held me up easily, pulling my back up against him.

He glared down at Nick.

"She never should have left the hospital," he growled, his voice furious. "I never thought her *friends* would let anyone take her out of there in that condition. Much less in order to handcuff her and grill her like a common criminal when she's loaded to the fucking gills on painkillers..." Pausing a beat as he continued to glower at Nick, he added more darkly, "You're never speaking to her in an official capacity again, if I have any say in it. Not without a lawyer. And I will sue this department into the stone ages if you pull anything like this again..."

"Mr. Black," Farraday spoke up, his voice warning.

206

I felt Black wanting to say more.

He was breathing harder, even as he fell silent.

His emotions crashed around me as he did, shocking me a little.

It hit me that this wasn't just an act, or even posturing to get at Nick. Black was furious — so angry he was having trouble controlling himself. Now that he was standing so close, gripping my arms in both of his hands, that anger practically bled through the pads of his fingers and the palms of his hands into my skin. That anger felt aimed almost solely at Nick.

He saw what Nick had done to me, bringing me down here, drugged and in shock and injured, as the worst kind of betrayal imaginable.

When I glanced at Nick himself, I saw a scowl touch his face.

Glancing at me, he leaned back, folding his arms.

Nick's expression remained closed, stone-faced as he looked away, focusing on the floor. Still, I saw something different there for the first time.

Something that looked a lot like guilt.

Then again, maybe I just wanted to see it.

BLACK CONTINUED TO SUPPORT ME, HOLDING MY ARMS IN HIS HANDS AS they led me out of the police station. He didn't speak to me again until we reached the street.

"You're staying with me tonight," he said, blunt.

I looked up, but I couldn't really see him from where he stood behind me.

"What?" I said, confused. "No. No... I just want to go home."

"You can't go home," he growled, gripping me tighter in his hands.

I watched a stretch limousine pull up to the curb next to us.

It occurred to me only then that Black and I now stood on the sidewalk alone. Farraday and Victoria White had walked away as soon as we hit the open air outside the station. When I craned my head and neck around, looking for them, I saw them walking and talking as they made their way up McAllister Street, presumably to return to their own cars.

The sky was lightening. When the realization hit me, I looked around with a dull surprise. I couldn't decide if I was surprised the night was over, or that it hadn't been over hours ago. It was still pre-dawn, but the sun was definitely on its way up.

I wasn't sure I had the energy to argue with Black.

"Good," he said.

"Why can't I go home?"

"It's not safe. And I'm not letting you go, Miriam, so drop it. It's my place or a hotel under armed guard... my people. Take your pick."

Nodding numbly, I didn't argue.

My mind started to turn over what Nick told me about Ian. I shoved that from my mind as well. I couldn't think about that now. I would think about that after I'd slept.

A chauffeur had gotten out of the driver's side of the limousine by then, and walked around to where we stood. Tipping his cap at the two of us, he gave me a concerned-seeming smile, right after he gave a much more deferential look to Black himself.

Then he was opening the back car door.

"Well?" Black said. "Where am I taking you, doc?"

I only exhaled, shrugging. "Wherever."

Letting out a relieved-sounding sigh, Black immediately began to steer me towards the open car door. I let him bring me inside, leaning on his proffered arm before I got in and pulled my hurt leg onto the white leather seat behind the rest of me. I found myself strangely relieved that I didn't have to explain more. I only sat there, my head leaned against the leather headrest, as Black walked around the back end of the car, not waiting for the driver but opening the door himself. He slid onto the back seat next to me.

"Take us home," he told the driver.

"Very good, sir."

I fell asleep before we even got there.

I had a vague memory of Black waking me when we arrived.

I had an even vaguer memory of being carried into an elevator... and then, after a blank-feeling pause, through a door I only vaguely recognized.

Not long after that, everything went blissfully dark once more.

That time, it stayed dark for a long time.

TWELVE
LOSS OF CONTROL

I WOKE UP CONFUSED, MY MEMORY DULL.

I was still so out of it, I didn't much care.

I also found myself distracted from trying to remember anything when I realized I wasn't alone. A body was pressed up against mine.

For a decent stretch of time, I didn't much care about that either.

Well, other than the fact that it was comfortably warm.

I must have fallen back asleep.

When I woke up the second time, my brain moved a little faster. Fast enough for the reality of that body to fully sink in.

I still didn't know where I was.

After a pause where I just lay there, thinking about that, I turned carefully, shifting my weight and head just enough to verify what I already knew.

Someone was definitely with me, holding me more or less in place. I didn't want to wake whoever it was, but I did want to know who they were. When I moved, trying to crane my head around to look, the arm around me tightened, pulling me deeper against him.

The tensed arm caused me to look down instead of back at his face.

The arm was entirely bare. Between that and the heat of his skin and feel of his chest against my back, I realized he wasn't wearing a shirt. Yet it wasn't Ian's arm I found myself looking at, or Ian's chest I felt against my back.

Tattoos ran down the inside of a more muscular and darker-toned left arm, including a large "S" on his forearm in black ink. I stared at that "S" mark for a long time for some reason, trying to decide what it meant. Next to it someone tattooed what looked almost like a serial number.

He had no scars that I could see, no marks at all except the recent ones from the other night, which consisted of a couple of cuts and bruises on his hand. The rest of his arm was untouched apart from those simple and somehow official-looking tattoos.

Studying the lean musculature, the even color of his skin around the tattoos, I didn't move for a long moment as my mind processed the fact he was even there. I was pretty sure I recognized the arm by then, from having seen it bare once before.

I at least recognized one of the rings he wore.

It was heavy brushed silver, with a set of rune-like patterns on the outside.

I was still looking at it, touching his fingers tentatively to turn it slightly so I could better examine the markings, when he pressed up against me, tightening his arm a second time.

That time, I felt a curl of heat go through me, catching in my chest.

Whatever it was, it didn't feel like it originated in me.

Before I could decide how to react to that, he tugged me further into the middle of the bed. I still hadn't yet made up my mind whether to resist when he pulled his own body out of the way, still tugging on me so that I shifted to my back. I found myself looking up at him, fighting the conflicting emotions running through me when I saw those gold eyes staring down.

I felt that heat on him intensify.

"How do you feel?" he said gruffly.

Closing my eyes, I looked away. I started to get up, but he didn't move out of my way to accommodate me. Catching hold of my wrists, he held me down instead.

"Relax. You're injured, doc. Don't get in a hurry."

I looked back up at him.

"What are you doing?" I said. "Here, I mean? With me?"

"Sharing light," he said at once.

"What? What does that mean?"

His jaw tightened. He shook his head perceptibly, but seemingly not in a no, or in frustration really. He didn't look away, but continued to stare down at my face. I saw his pupils visibly dilate and swallowed, feeling a wash of nerves go through me in spite of myself.

"It's a seer thing," he said, his voice still gruff. "It should help you heal faster."

"From this... sharing light?" I said. I tried lamely to insert humor in my voice and only half-succeeded. "And that required you to be in bed with me? Shirtless?"

His eyes flickered over my face. "Yes," he said.

The silence between us deepened.

I started to get up again, but he held me there, gripping my wrists.

"Relax."

"Am I a prisoner here?" I said, exasperated.

I still wasn't afraid of him for some reason.

"You hurt your leg," he said.

"I'm aware of that. Does that mean I can't use the bathroom?"

"That's not why you want to get up," he said.

Swallowing, I stared up at his face. He was right. I didn't really want to think about the implications of his observation, but I knew he was right.

My mind went to Ian. But I didn't want to think about Ian either, or what Nick had told me the night before, which I now remembered, even if some of the details were still fuzzy.

I remembered the gist.

Ian lied to me.

More than lied, he'd treated me like one of his damned interrogations for his job, like I was a spy behind enemy lines. And yes, I'd been lying to him too, so maybe I deserved it. Maybe he even had a right to do it, if he'd been worried about me like Nick said.

Maybe, like Nick, Ian thought I was being manipulated by a psychopath.

Even so, I couldn't believe Ian had done what he did... or maybe just that he'd done it the way he did it. I knew we'd been having problems lately, and miscommunications, and yes, honesty issues... but I couldn't believe he'd resort to running a game on me rather than asking me outright what the hell was going on, at least once he'd brought me outside. Even with Ian's job, I never would have believed it of him.

Moreover, if he was that worried about me, why had he left me with Black at all? To see if I'd sleep with him? To see if I'd feel guilty and call him, confess my sins like I'd contemplated doing as I stood outside the Cliff House door?

I'd never wanted to believe that we could be that couple. The game-playing, entrapping one another, spying on one another couple.

I never would have done anything like that to him.

Well, I thought to myself. *Probably not.*

I tried to decide if that would be true if I'd suspected Ian of an affair.

I'd always been the one who struggled with jealousy... not Ian. I was the one who had to fight to be rational, to act like an adult when it came to my feelings. Ian was Mr. Rational. That was part of the reason I told myself Ian was good for me; he helped me to think before I spoke, to put reason before feeling. When I was a kid I'd been so out of control. Outbursts, tantrums, irrational anger and jealousy. I'd gotten in fights. I'd worked most of my adult life to develop a cooler exterior, to be able to present my feelings logically.

Normally, Ian helped with that.

Now this rationality of his struck me as a bit cold.

Maybe mine had gotten pretty cold, too.

I found myself remembering Zoe, how dumb she thought it was that I was always trying to control my emotions. Being sixteen, she mocked me for "playing grown-up," and "acting like mom." Zoe was more like our dad. Unapologetic. Spontaneous. Quick to anger but also quick to laugh. Affectionate.

Yet dad had always worried about me... not Zoe.

Dad thought *I* was the one who was too volatile.

Thinking about that now, it struck me as strange.

I knew I was still distracting myself from Black though, whose stare I could still feel. I tried to think about Ian objectively instead, to put myself in Ian's shoes, but I knew at least some of that was avoidance, too. I tried to decide how I really felt about him, but I couldn't make up my mind about that either.

Whatever his reasons for doing what he did, I couldn't think about it now.

215

I needed to ask Ian those questions personally.

"I can't be here," I told Black, looking up. "I need to go home."

He shook his head, once. "It's not safe."

I let out an incredulous laugh. "From who?"

"The killer," he said. "Give me more time, Miriam. A few more hours. Stay with me until we ID him for real. Then you can go home."

I gave him an impatient look, meeting his gaze. "Now who's lying?"

"I can have multiple reasons for saying something without lying," he said, no apology in his voice. "And I do have people looking for him right now. Which is all that matters."

When I exhaled, half in exasperation, he pressed up against me again.

That time, I closed my eyes. I couldn't help it, or the flush of reaction that heated my skin.

Glancing up, I felt my jaw tighten as he watched my face. I felt that heat on him intensify more, the longer he stared at me, right before he lowered his mouth.

"Don't," I said, turning my head.

He raised his head at once.

I felt more of him though. Enough of him seemed to snake around me that I was having trouble thinking about or feeling anything else. Heat lived in that wash of presence. Heat, but not only that. The feeling there caught in my chest, making it hard to breathe. I felt emotion in that heat, longing, a pain that slid through the very pores of my skin, pulling on me like a physical force. It brought a strange mix of nausea and discomfort, most of that centered in my chest and belly. My hands curled into fists as the feeling worsened.

I realized whatever it was, it was making me more emotional, too.

"What the hell is that?" I said finally. "What are you doing to me?"

I looked up when he didn't answer right away.

I studied his face, noting the hardness of his features as he looked at me.

I want you, a voice murmured in my head.

I let out a disbelieving laugh. "No shit. It's not gonna happen, Black."

Please.

"Absolutely not."

"Why not?" he said aloud.

I met his gaze, biting my lip at the expression there. He'd lowered his face somewhere in that, so that he was only a few inches away from my mouth again.

"You know why," I blurted, fighting to hold his stare. "I told you why... yesterday..."

"Is that still the reason?"

"That I'm engaged?" I said, disbelieving. "Why wouldn't it be?"

"Because you want me, too." That heat on him intensified once more, making my eyes close as my breathing sped up. "You were pulling on me all night. You're pulling on me right now, doc." He pressed his forehead against mine, his voice a murmur, "And you're having doubts about him. About your man... the one you were going to marry..."

"The one I *am* going to marry." Moving my head away, I glared up at him.

"If you say so, doc."

He pressed against me deliberately, sensually, his jaw

217

tightening as his weight grew heavier. I let out an involuntary gasp. Before I realized I meant to, I pressed against him in return, unable to help myself when I felt his erection.

His eyes closed, right before he let out a low sound.

"Gods... you want me. I can feel it... it's driving me fucking crazy..."

"No," I said. I shook my head. "I don't want you. You're wrong."

I didn't sound wholly convinced though, even to my own ears.

I had one hand on his chest, ostensibly holding him up and back, but I wasn't really pushing on him, or even creating much resistance. I definitely wasn't trying to get him off me.

I found myself feeling his heart under my palm and fingers instead, noticing there was something strange about it, and not only because it was beating harder the longer I stroked him there. The muscles of his chest were strangely perfect, his skin unblemished even for a man much younger than him. I felt another, stronger wash of that heat and pain off him and bit my lip, hard enough to taste blood.

"Fuck," he said, watching me. "Fuck... tell me something... anything..."

When I looked up, that pain had reached his eyes, softening his expression. His eyes grew more glassed as he watched me look at him.

"Say no like you mean it, at least." He kissed the side of my face, pressing his cheek against mine. He leaned into me with his face, rubbing it against my neck. "Tell me no again, and I'll listen, Miriam..." he murmured. "I promise."

He raised his head, once more looking down at my eyes.

I couldn't hold his gaze.

Swallowing, I looked back at his chest, then at his arms tensed on either side of his body where he held himself up. I fought to think. I felt him pushing at me with his mind, trying to get an answer out of me... but I didn't feel any manipulation or guile there. I felt intensity instead, woven into the question even behind what had to be self-restraint. I fought with that pull — a pull so strong I almost couldn't think past it now.

There was something there. Something I didn't understand.

And yet... all I needed to say was no.

He was listening for it, waiting for it.

I could feel that he meant it, that some part of him felt guilty for how hard he was pushing me now. That alienness lived there too; I couldn't push either thing out of my awareness entirely, or the fact that he felt strangely young as he hung over me.

Not young. Nervous. I was making him nervous again.

When I looked up that time, he studied my face carefully.

When I nodded, barely perceptible, he let out a low gasp.

He lowered his mouth, kissing me before I could think that through, either. His mouth was soft; in seconds he used his lips to part mine, then his tongue was exploring my mouth and he was doing that thing he'd accused me of doing... *pulling* on me in some way.

It felt like some part of him was pulling me out of my own mind.

It definitely felt like he was pulling me into him... away from myself... even as he put more of himself into me. Feeling his presence flood into me, I gasped against his mouth and he groaned, gripping my hair in his hand as he kissed me harder.

Something about that kiss completely shut off my brain.

I don't mean only in relation to Ian.

I think I forgot about everything about then.

He pressed his entire weight into me as the kiss continued, and that intensity on him worsened, making me lose touch with the room.

When he raised his head next, some undetermined chunk of time later, he was lying between my legs, leaning on the thigh that hadn't been hurt, maybe to keep himself off the bandaged one. One of his arms and hands was wrapped around my back, his fingers fisting my hair. The other hand was under my shirt, stroking my skin, pausing to massage muscle and trace bones. I'd barely noticed him doing it, although I shivered now under his touch. My own fingers gripped his hair. I kissed the sides of his mouth, caressing his jaw with my fingertips.

I wanted him. I wanted him... God, he was right.

I'd wanted him practically since we'd first met.

The realization scared me.

Guilt flooded into me, blanking out my mind in a different way. I tried to pull my thoughts back together, to make sense of what I was doing.

I tried to think about Ian.

I tried to think about whether I should stop this.

I tried to make myself want to.

Black kissed me again, harder, pressing his body against mine.

He was sending me pictures then, images so sharp I winced.

Then that heat flooded into me more, dimming my doubts all over again.

I felt the question behind the images. I felt it, but pretended I didn't.

Then he was pushing up my shirt, kissing more of me as he slid down my body. I didn't even pretend to fight him that time. I felt drugged... like something about him drugged me... or maybe something about the two of us together. I closed my eyes as he pulled off the sweat pants and then my underwear carefully, moving them cautiously over my injured leg before yanking them the rest of the way off my calves and feet almost roughly.

Then his fingers were inside me and I moaned.

He had his mouth on me seconds later and my brain fuzzed out again, unable to think past what he was doing. That pain in him worsened, even as his fingers circled my wrist, holding it down on the bed. I still had my other hand in his hair, gripping him tightly enough I had to be hurting him. I felt his pain from that too, but it only intensified that other heat, turning him on more. He had his fingers inside me again as he lowered his mouth.

I honestly have no idea how long he was doing that.

My mind shifted to the blond he'd had in here the day before, what she'd said to me as he led her out. Jealousy nearly blanked out my brain, shocking me with its intensity, much less the fact that I felt it at all.

For some reason, he got off on that, too.

I felt that heat radiating off him intensify even though— briefly at least—I had to restrain the impulse not to hit him in the face.

He got me to talk to him at one point. He stopped me from coming, demanding I talk to him to get him to go back to what he'd been doing.

He did that again. And again.

I felt glimmers of insecurity or maybe doubt on him in that, or maybe just that echo of my first no. I felt his pain worsen alongside mine when I finally begged him, gripping his hair in my fist.

I came not long after that.

I lost it completely when I did, bucking involuntarily up against his mouth.

I don't think I had a single thought in my head by then.

Even so, those more intense emotions were crashing into me harder, blinding me with their intensity. Most of those weren't his. They were mine. Feelings about Zoe. Feelings about my parents, my life... the war... Ian... Nick... those murdered girls. Confusion around Black. I fought to control the emotion that caught in my chest, and the mere fact of doing so made me realize just how long I'd been fighting to control those feelings.

With Ian. With my friends, my family.

I felt Black fighting with that control even now, fighting to get me to open.

He brought me to a second orgasm before I'd come down from the first, and then he slid his body back up next to mine so that he was lying on me again, still carefully avoiding my hurt leg. I was studying his face when he caught hold of the bottom of my shirt, pulling it up over my head and working it off my arms. He tossed it on the floor once he had me free of it.

Then he was staring at the rest of me, that pain on him worsening.

He'd gotten naked somewhere in that too. I didn't notice until he pressed down his weight—then I groaned aloud, feeling him against my inner thigh.

I felt him wanting me to look at him.

When I didn't, he let out a low groan of his own.

"Look at me..." he gasped. "We're different, Miriam. Look at me."

I glanced up at him, fighting that pain in my chest as I bit my lip.

"Look at my cock... look at me, Miriam... my body..."

He felt softer somehow in the request, almost vulnerable.

That strange pain on him grew more intense, the one that felt more like desire and longing than real pain. Again, images flickered through my mind, that time of him inside me, fucking me. I closed my eyes, biting my lip, but I couldn't get away from it, or from the feelings pluming off him in hotter clouds as he let himself go into the fantasy. If anything the images themselves only grew clearer without his real face and body to intervene.

When his feelings rose... mine did too, until I couldn't breathe again.

"Stop..." I begged him. My voice wavered. "Please."

I felt him pull it back with an effort.

"It might hurt," he said, his voice a gasp. "The first time... just the first time. It might hurt, Miriam, but only that one time... then it will feel so fucking good... so good... for both of us." That pain on him worsened, forcing him briefly silent. "I want you to know what you're getting yourself into. You need to look at me, Miriam."

I felt the wanting there, so intensely it blanked out everything else.

More than just wanting, loneliness lived there, a wanting of contact... God, he wanted to be inside me so badly he was barely controlling himself.

Something about knowing that worsened my desire to the point of complete irrationality. I felt him fighting that loss of control, half out of his head as he struggled to talk himself down. Some part of me didn't even want him to talk himself down. I felt that more animalistic part of him fighting the rest of him, saw it behind his eyes. That part of him just wanted to hold me down, to fuck me until I understood him. I felt him wanting that, even trying to rationalize it to himself, why it would be all right.

223

That wanting stabbed through me, once more choking off my own rational thought.

Not just sex. He wanted to be with someone like him.

He so desperately wanted to be with someone like him.

Fighting back that impulse to end the conversation, to just give in to what he wanted, he used his mind to show me another image instead, until it dominated the rest.

It was an image of his cock, I realized.

The realization managed to jerk my mind off pulling on him, trying to get him to lose control.

He looked different from any man I'd ever seen—or any boy, for that matter.

Longer, thicker, his sex organ had more of a triangular tip than the mushroom-shaped ones I associated with other men. But it wasn't just the difference in the curve, or the differences in his shape. A smaller, sharp-looking, thorn-like... something... came out of the end while I watched from my mind's eye. Whatever it was, it emerged from right below where the urethra lived on most men. It didn't look quite like flesh.

It looked almost like cartilage.

I gasped, my hands gripping his chest as I stared at it.

"Hirik," he said, his voice gruff. "We call it *hirik*... it's normal for us, Miriam."

That time, real fear writhed through me.

It was enough to snap me out of that fugue state at least.

He must have felt me pulling away from him. He must have felt at least part of my brain turning back on from wherever it was we'd both gone.

"I won't hurt you more than I have to," he promised, his voice cajoling, reassuring. He pressed against me again, groaning as images of being inside me once more flooded his mind. "Don't be afraid of me, Miriam... please. It'll only hurt the one time. I swear it."

He closed his eyes, and the desire on him grew so intense I let out an involuntary whimper, writhing under him, grasping his biceps with both hands. He groaned, pressing against me as his voice grew almost hoarse.

"It'll be *so much better* after. Gods, Miriam... so much better. Better than sex with humans. I promise you... I promise you, Miriam." He shook his head, gripping my hips in both of his hands, and I realized he was sweating, that he was so turned on his body had completely softened over me as he pressed against me. "I promise you'll like it... I promise... and I'll do whatever you want. Anything, Miriam. Anything... I'll give you anything you want..."

I felt the truth there.

I heard him begging too, which brought back that fog of desire, making it impossible to think or even see him clearly. He wasn't lying to me, not knowingly anyway. I believed him somehow, even though a part of me couldn't wrap my head around any of it in terms of logistics. He didn't want to hurt me. He wanted me to be okay with this.

Some part of me spun around what we'd already done, how lost in this I already was.

That emotional intensity still burned there, in my chest. Foreign... but also not foreign. It was me. It was definitely me. I'd just forgotten it was me, somehow.

I thought about how different Black was... normally, I mean.

When he wasn't begging me for sex.

That fear worsened, growing unbearable.

I remembered Ian.

I couldn't. I couldn't do this.

"Stop," I managed, pushing on his chest for real that time. "Get off me. Black, get off me... please..."

He obeyed.

I felt the split-second of hesitation before he did, right before that pain coming off him worsened exponentially. He rolled to his right and my left, landing on his back on the mattress, gasping as he gripped the sheets in his hands.

For a long moment, neither of us made a sound apart from breathing.

I moved away from him once I could.

"Gods," he said, half a groan. He looked up at me as I slid my legs to the side of the bed, his gold eyes so glassy I wondered if he could see me at all. "Don't leave. Miriam... don't. Please. I won't touch you if you don't want me to..."

I winced at his tone.

That pain wove into his words, pulling on me like an electrical force.

Worse, it brought the emotion back, nearly bringing tears to my eyes.

But I was already halfway to my feet.

He didn't move as I got up... or as I grabbed my clothes off the bed and the floor, gritting my teeth at the pain in my leg. I only paused long enough to pull my shirt over my head, balling the sweatpants up in my hands once I was mostly covered. I grabbed my underwear off the floor too, feeling myself flush as I crushed the gauzy fabric inside my fist.

I didn't look at him again before I walked out of the room.

I told myself I'd stopped because of Ian. I told myself I *had* to stop, that I couldn't do this, not without talking to Ian first. I couldn't make myself believe it, though.

The realization only made me feel more guilty.

Black didn't follow me into the other room.

I finished dressing in his living room, even as I looked around for my bag, for money or anything I could use to get the hell out of there. I found my purse on the bar in his kitchen, right where I'd left it the day before, complete with my car and house keys, my ticket stub for the parking garage and even my wallet. I'd left all of that behind when we took Black's helicopter across the city, mostly because Black advised me to leave it here.

He seemed to think it would be better if I didn't have identification on me.

Since I'd known I needed to come back to California Street for my car anyway, and Black clearly didn't need my money, I'd felt pretty safe leaving it behind. I'd brought cash with me instead, but I couldn't remember spending any of that either, apart from a bottle of water I bought at the Legion of Honor café.

It was hard to believe that had been less than twenty-four hours ago.

Grabbing my purse off the granite counter, I looked around for my shoes.

Those, I couldn't find.

After a few times of circling his living room and checking the few closets I found, I decided I didn't care. Not enough to go back to the bedroom to look for them.

I wasn't thrilled about walking on the city streets barefoot, but I'd survive.

Driving barefoot didn't bother me. I'd done it before.

I could feel Black recovering in that other room. That pulling sensation hadn't stopped, but I felt his restraint lock back into place, which was probably what kept him from following me.

I knew neither thing would last, though.

He'd follow me into the living room soon enough, and he'd

want to talk. If I knew myself or him at all by now, I had to get the hell out of there before that happened. If I didn't, we'd probably end up having sex on his living room floor.

As I thought it, that pain in my chest worsened.

Enough to let me know he'd heard me thinking that, too.

Miriam, he murmured in my mind. *Please, don't leave. Please.*

I didn't answer.

It's not safe...

I let out a humorless laugh, once more inexplicably fighting tears. *I think it's pretty obviously not safe for me here either, Black.*

I felt him fighting for self-control again. I wondered if it was what I'd said. Then I realized it was from me speaking to him in his mind at all.

He felt the emotion there, too.

Let me send a car at least...

I fought back and forth with that. Then I shook my head. *No. I need my car.*

A ride to the parking structure then. My people can follow you home...

Black, I warned. *I'll be fine. You know Nick'll have people here... people who'll see me leave. They'll follow me home.*

I swallowed as the truth of that sank in, and the fact that Nick would know already that I'd spent the night here, at Black's penthouse. I wondered if he'd tell Ian. Shoving that out of my mind, I shook my head.

No one's going to try and break into my place, all right? Not now. Not with half the cops in the city watching me and you...

I'll lock myself in the bathroom, he offered, even as that pulling sensation strengthened in my chest. *I'll masturbate.* His desire worsened, enough that I felt my heart stutter. *I'll hire a fucking prostitute. Don't leave, Miriam... please. Please...*

228

But I was already standing in front of the door to his penthouse apartment.

Gripping the purse against my chest with one arm, I fought to control my breathing.

At his mention of hiring a prostitute, I gritted my teeth.

Then I reached out with my hand and grasped the handle, jerking open the door.

That time, I didn't look back.

THIRTEEN

LOSING MY RELIGION

D RIVING WAS HORRIBLE. I'D FORGOTTEN ABOUT NEEDING MY LEG to work the clutch, which was its own kind of hell. For the first time in my life, I wondered why in name of all that is holy I still drove a manual stick-shift car. I'd always driven one, but until now, it never struck me as having some real disadvantages. But every time I used the gear shift and clutch on the way back to my apartment, fire shot up my whole leg, making me grit my teeth in agony.

The fact that it was San Francisco meant I couldn't exactly avoid upshifting and downshifting for long periods of time, either.

On the plus side, I actually found parking.

I lucked out, managing to get back to my neighborhood right at the end of street cleaning in front of my building for that day. Because of that, most of the slots weren't yet re-filled from people moving their cars to avoid the expensive tickets.

Well, apart from one unlucky truck owner who had the tell-tale yellow envelope stuck under his wiper blade already.

Limping up to my building, I sorted my keys in one hand even as I kept my eyes trained on the pavement, skirting around broken glass and anything else that might slice open my bare feet. The sidewalk was relatively clear, thank goodness, and I stuck my key into the front lock a minute or so later, pausing only to stare at the unmarked white van I saw parked on the corner.

Nick's people? It had to be.

I only hoped they hadn't bugged my place.

Remembering I'd promised Ian I was going to stop by his place that morning, a wave of depression fell over me. I was dreading talking to Ian, and not only because I had no idea if he'd continue the charade he'd begun last night.

I guessed he probably wouldn't. He'd likely talked to Nick again by now.

Either way, I don't think I'd ever felt so bad about myself. I knew I wasn't always the best girlfriend in the world, but I'd never cheated on one of my partners before. Truthfully, I'd never even come close before today.

I wondered if Nick knew by now that he'd been lied to by Ian as well, that Ian really had been in San Francisco last night.

I wasn't sure if I wanted to know all the cloak and dagger logistics though.

At this point, I felt like I was on pretty shaky ground in terms of yelling at Ian for much of anything, no matter what lies he'd told. Still, it was pretty clear we had a lot bigger problems than I'd realized, and about a lot more serious, foundational things than Ian's overly-frequent business trips. That depressed me as much as the actual cheating, I think.

More, maybe.

I sighed as I jerked the key inside the sticky lock, jiggling it a few times before I managed to turn it counter-clockwise to open the outer security door. Once I got through it, I checked my mailbox in rote, emptying it out before I began to trudge up the stairs to my two-bedroom flat on the fifth floor. I found myself thinking mostly about a shower now.

A really hot shower...to be followed by bed.

Well, maybe a really hot shower, a cup of coffee, a call to Ian, and then bed.

I really couldn't put off calling Ian any longer.

I was still pulling myself laboriously up the stairs, using the bannister, when something else occurred to me. I no longer had my phone. Truthfully, I had no idea where my phone even was at this point. It could have been burned in the fire. Black might have it from when he collected me from the police station. Or Nick might have it in an evidence bag somewhere, to be examined by his tech team when they got to it.

I hadn't had a land line in years.

That meant I'd either have to go pick up a burner phone somewhere, probably at one of the corner drug stores, or drive by Ian's house to talk to him in person.

Either option sounded exhausting.

Even so, I found myself thinking maybe it was better. I needed to talk to Ian in person, given everything. I'd planned to ask him to come by my place later, since I wasn't overly mobile, but maybe it was better if I went to him.

Maybe it was better if I did it soon, too.

I'd just reached the top landing as I made up my mind to go immediately after I showered and changed. I knew enough about injuries to know it was probably better to keep moving if I wanted to do it today. If I let my leg stiffen up too much, it would be agony to get out the door again later.

I was standing at the top of the landing as I thought it, pulling out my keys. I stared at the set, looking for the smaller, silver one for my front door...

When someone cleared their throat.

I dropped the keys, startled. They hit the mottled brown rug.

Bending down, the bannister clutched in one white-knuckled hand, I didn't take my eyes off the man standing there.

He gave me a faint smile. "You look like you've seen a ghost, Miri."

"Ian." Grasping the keys off the floor, I straightened, wincing as I did. "I was just thinking about you."

"Pity not enough to call me."

I frowned, letting my eyes drop back to my key set as I limped towards where he stood in the alcove by my doorway, leaning against the wall.

"I don't have my phone," I said, deciding not to explain further.

I heard him frown, but I didn't look up to confirm.

"I brought coffee," he said, his voice artificially light, although I clearly heard the edge. "Of course, I got here two hours ago, after giving up on you coming to visit me...so it's likely cold as fucking ice."

I pressed my lips together, but didn't answer as I inserted the key into the deadbolt of my door.

"What happened to your leg?" he asked, his voice colder.

"Shrapnel from a bomb," I told him flatly.

He didn't speak as I finished turning the stiff lock with my silver key. When I glanced up at him as I swung the door inward to my Victorian apartment, I saw him staring at me. The hostility in his eyes hadn't disappeared, or even faded much.

"Shrapnel?" he said. "Is that a joke?"

I exhaled in anger. "Are you seriously going to pretend you haven't been talking to Nick?" I said. "Jesus, Ian. I thought you'd drop the act by now."

"Nick?" He stared at me. Then his blue eyes narrowed. "Why would I have been talking to Nick? Is that where you were all night? With Nick? Because I thought..."

He cut off his own words, as if biting them back.

"...I assumed you were with that other fellow," he said, folding his arms tightly across his chest. His voice came out more subdued that time, but also colder, almost gruff. "The 'client' I met last night. Whatever his name was. Black."

Exhaling more in weariness than anger, I entered my apartment, leaving the door wide open behind me for him to follow.

Combing my fingers through my tangled hair, I dumped my purse on the low table by my coat closet along with my mail and limped towards the kitchen.

"Coffee?" I said.

"Tea."

I glanced over as he dumped two coffees in a cardboard holder into my trash, taking his foot off the lid pedal so that the cover fell down with a smack.

Averting my gaze, I filled the kettle all the way to the top and put it on to boil.

Then I walked to the fridge and opened the freezer door, pulling out my cache of espresso beans. Dumping a bunch in my scuffed and grounds-dusted coffee grinder, I wrapped the rubber band back around the bag and tossed it in the freezer before fitting the cap over the top of the grinder.

By the time the tea kettle began to whistle, I had the filter set up over my cup, the beans ground to a fine, moist powder.

235

Another cup held a bag of Ian's high-end brand of Earl Grey, which I kept a box of in my cupboard.

It was low-tech, but it worked for me, living alone.

A few minutes later, I hobbled over to the kitchen table with both cups, setting the tea down in front of where Ian sat. He'd already taken his usual seat staring into the living room behind me, versus the one facing the windows that I always preferred.

I remembered the two of us joking in the past that we were perfectly suited because our instincts always drew us in opposite directions.

The joke struck me as pretty hollow now.

I took a sip of the strong coffee I'd already laced with milk.

"So?" Ian said, his voice holding impatience now. "Who goes first?"

I looked up, realizing only then that I'd been twisting the engagement ring around my finger in a nervous tic. One of the oldest tells in the world, according to my psych books. I saw Ian's eyes locked on my fingers where I'd been doing it and stopped at once.

Realizing that the rest of it was just song and dance, I cut to the chase.

"I don't think we should get married," I told him.

Silence. I felt my jaw harden as I stared out the window, right before I looked back at his face. His expression had gone utterly cold, like a wooden mask.

When I didn't say anything else for a few seconds longer, he met my gaze.

"That's it?" he said, his voice even harder. "Do I get to know why?"

I felt my fingers tighten as I stared down at my mug of coffee.

"I almost slept with Black," I said. Then, remembering his

mouth on me, my hand fisted in his hair as I came violently against him, I felt my jaw harden more. "I *did* sleep with him," I amended, feeling a curl of shame. "More or less. I imagine you'd view it as more."

The silence between us turned almost physical.

"I'm sorry," I said. I stared down at my hands wrapped around the mug. Staring at the ring I still wore, I felt that sick feeling of shame in my gut worsen. "I didn't plan on it. It wasn't..." I waved vaguely over my mug. "...planned. It wasn't planned, Ian."

Realizing how inadequate that was, I bit my lip, if only to force myself to stop talking.

It occurred to me that I might be being crueler about this than I'd ever intended. I didn't want to hurt him. I felt like hell about hurting him, but I also didn't know how to soft-pedal this and still be honest.

I probably shouldn't have tried to talk about this at all right now, truthfully. My brain wasn't operating on all four cylinders, and I knew it. Especially with how tired I was. Especially after everything that had happened in the last three days.

In the same breath, I realized I was angry with Ian too.

"Why did you lie to me?" I said, looking up. "Can you tell me that, at least?"

Ian continued to stare out the window, his eyes focused blankly to his right.

From the direction of his stare, he appeared to be focusing on the row of apartment buildings opposite mine, but he didn't seem to be seeing anything. Truthfully, I doubted he knew where he was focused.

From his face, I couldn't be sure he'd heard me, either.

"You told Nick you were still in Bangkok last night," I

prompted, gripping my coffee mug tighter in my hands. "You pretended with me that you didn't know who Black was...that you'd never heard his name before..."

"What makes you think I had?"

His voice startled me into silence.

Then I shook my head, feeling my frown deepen.

"Ian," I said. "Nick told me. He told me you said you were in Bangkok last night. He said you claimed to be working—"

"Working," he said. "Yes. I suppose I did say that."

He folded his arms, leaning back in the wooden chair. He stared at me, and still, his eyes were so distant I couldn't read anything in his face.

I couldn't be sure he was seeing me, even now.

"I suppose I wasn't," he said. "...Working. Not in the way I implied."

The silence returned.

For some reason, I was getting more angry with him, not less.

Maybe that was just defensive, too.

"Meaning what?" I said finally.

His gaze sharpened as he stared at me. I still didn't see much of him in it though.

"Meaning I did go to the Cliff House for business," he said, abrupt. "...Unlike what I told you last night. At the time, I thought it was to assess an enemy agent, whose phone I'd traced back to that location. Rather, that business ended with me watching my *fiancée*..." He hit the word hard enough to make me flinch, right before he glared at me from across the table. "...being openly seduced by that same person. A man I now know to be a spy."

"A spy?" I let out an involuntary laugh. "Black? A spy?"

"You heard me." His voice grew colder as he leaned towards

238

me. "He's a traitor, Miriam. So I wouldn't grow too fond of him, if I were you. You know what they do to traitors, don't you?"

Pausing deliberately, he leaned back in his chair, firming his mouth.

"You're not a stupid woman. Given that, perhaps you have your own theories about why he might have targeted you?"

I felt my shame turn into something else.

Something a lot closer to real anger, even as my hands curled into fists.

"First he's a serial killer...now he's a goddamned spy?" I said. "Are you kidding me right now? Did Nick put you up to this?"

"I've always told you there was a danger someone would use you to get to me."

I found myself turning over his words, fighting to think about them.

Nick said Black was overly interested in Ian. That he seemed to know too much about him, and about what he did for a living. Further, Black had a background in intelligence. I'd never doubted that, even apart from all of his gadgets and his ability to get gun permits at a moment's notice from the DOJ.

Even so, something about Ian's explanation struck a different kind of warning note in me.

"Are you threatening him?" I said incredulously. "Black?"

"It wouldn't be me making the decision, Miri."

"That's not what I asked!"

"I'm not a threat to Black," he said coldly. "But my employers might be. They don't tend to look very favorably upon traitors and terrorists."

Still giving him a faintly disbelieving look, I shook my head, lowering my coffee cup after taking a long sip. "I'm sorry, Ian. I don't believe that. I don't know what you were really doing at the Cliff House last night, but—"

"Are you seriously going to tell me there's absolutely nothing wrong with him, Miriam?" Ian's eyes met mine when I turned, so cold I barely recognized the man I knew there. "Really? Is that what you're telling me? That Black's just a run of the mill private dick...?" His voice grew even more biting. "...Just like *you're* a run of the mill psychologist?"

I stared at him. Wariness slid through me, enough that I studied his face openly.

"What in the hell is that supposed to mean?"

He leaned over the table, his eyes ice-blue.

"You just had to fucking *sleep* with the bastard, didn't you?" he hissed, planting his hands on the table. "You just couldn't *help* yourself, is that it, Miriam? How did it happen...being as 'unplanned' as you say? You just accidentally fell on his cock after you *accidentally* found yourself in his bed? Is that how it went?"

I felt my fingers tighten once more on the mug.

Even so, that thread of distrust I'd felt the night before, the one I'd ignored in favor of trusting the man I'd thought I would spend the rest of my life with, grew prominent in my mind again. That trust unraveled further the longer I looked at him.

Distrust wound through me around Black too, but it was different with him. Weirdly, when it came to some things, I trusted Black more.

Something else hit me in the same set of seconds.

Black hadn't wanted me to come here, to my apartment. He'd practically begged me to stay there with him, to wait until his people found the location of the killer before I returned home. And sure, he'd wanted sex, but that hadn't been all of it.

Black really seemed to think it wasn't safe for me here.

But why? *Why* would Black have thought that? Why would Black think the killer even knew who I was, much less where I lived?

A cold finger pricked down my spine.

I knew why.

The truth of it stared me directly in the face. Really it had been there all along, ever since Black entered my life, only I'd been too dense to see it.

Ian.

Black had been tracking Ian.

Even as I thought it, my breath stopped, stuck in my chest as the puzzle pieces drifted down, falling into place behind my eyes. Black hadn't only been asking questions about me that day at the police station. He'd been asking questions about Ian. Moreover, Nick told me that Black had known things about Ian — things he shouldn't have known, not if Black's only connection to Ian was through me.

Nick interpreted that as Black screwing with him... thumbing his nose at the police, or even as Black being jealous of Ian because of me. But looking at it now, I realized neither thing was true. Black hadn't primarily been there to learn about me at all. I was a side project for him, a distraction, maybe even an unexpected bonus.

Black let himself get arrested so he could grill the police about the *rogue seer* he'd been chasing...not about me.

Remembering Ian and Black sizing one another up at the Cliff House, and the look on each man's face as they'd stared the other down, I couldn't help feeling the similarity there. Ian definitely hid it better than Black, but I could clearly see the strangeness there, too — that odd sense of difference mirrored in each man, if in separate and almost opposite ways. Moreover, it explained why Ian bothered to spar with Black at all. Unlike what I'd thought, that hadn't been about me either. It had been about Black himself.

Ian saw Black as his equal.

Like a peer.

Once it all clicked, I couldn't un-see it.

That fear in my chest worsened, catching my breath.

Black suspected Ian. He'd suspected him all along. Which meant he thought Ian might be the Wedding Killer, too.

And Black hadn't told me because...well, because he was Black. I didn't know his exact reasons, but maybe he'd wanted to be sure first. He'd implied that was the reason, that he wanted to be sure, that he wanted a positive ID on the killer before we did anything else. It occurred to me too, that Black might have been keeping me close in part to draw Ian out.

Or maybe even to protect me.

Impulsively, I opened my mind. I hadn't tried to read Ian since the first week we met, and that had just been a precaution, a few light dust-overs to make sure Ian was who he said he was. But I needed to know. I needed to know the truth.

At first, I got nothing really.

Muttered words, images...a lot of anger, which I expected.

I got a bare whisper that went deeper than anger...

Malice.

Feeling that, I flinched.

I probed deeper, pushing harder than maybe I ever had before.

The malice deepened, grew more devious.

Hatred. Disgust. Then...

Jealousy. So much jealousy. Hatred of Black. Wanting him

dead, cut up, his cock chopped off, his face slashed. Hatred of me. Hatred that he cared. *So much hatred* that he cared at all what I'd done to him.

Dirty whore halfbreed bitch...

Spiral cuts, a silver-handled tool shaped almost like a brand...

A shadow loomed over me.

I moved in instinct, feeling the danger.

I didn't move fast enough.

Ian lunged over the table at me even as I jerked violently backwards. My chair's back slammed into the wall as he grabbed my throat in both of his hands, dragging me towards him.

Panicking, I threw my whole weight back, trying to break free, but he squeezed his fingers so hard he cut off my breath.

I fought to stand, swinging at him, but my bad leg buckled.

Before my mind could wrap around what was happening, he was dragging me over the table.

He punched me in the face on the way there, knocking over our mugs, a vase, burning my leg on the coffee I'd only barely started to drink. Then he had me on the other side, where he hit me again, twice, stunning me.

The next thing I knew, both of his hands were locked around my throat.

I hung there, choking.

He held me up against the wall and part of the window frame. My fingers clutched at the thicker ones wrapped around my neck, my toes barely scraping the floor.

I kicked out at him with my good leg.

Then I writhed in his hold, hitting out at him with elbows and knees, in a blind panic to get free. My hands wrapped more desperately around his fingers where they squeezed my throat, trying to get under them, and he slammed my head against the wall, hard enough that I saw white.

The blow stunned me, nearly knocked me out.

I dragged in breaths, fighting to get oxygen into my lungs before I blacked out for real. Giving bare gasps, I looked around for a weapon, anything, gripping his fingers tighter.

Knives in the kitchen...too far. Wine bottle candle holder. Stone lion my friend Lacey brought back for me from Africa... spare keys...a book...

My mind fuzzed when he squeezed harder.

He lowered his head, bringing his lips to my ear.

"Say something clever, Miri," he hissed softly. "Go on. Astound me with that amazing half-worm intellect of yours. Or better yet...why don't you try again to use your pathetic, halfbreed sight against mine?" He slammed my head against the wall again and I let out a groan, my eyes rolling up. "I thought you had rules about that kind of thing, pet? Do I fall outside them now? Is it open season on me now that you have another *brother seer* to suck off...?"

"Ian," I gasped. "Ian...I'm sorry...I'm sorry..."

"Yeah. I bet you are. I just bet you're sorry *now*, Miri."

He leaned closer to me, smelling my hair.

"...I can smell him all over you, Miriam. I smelled him out in the damned hallway. So how did he like it? Did he enjoy rolling in the filth of your half-breed cunt...?"

I stared up at him, confused.

He'd said it a few times though. He clearly wanted me to hear it.

Half-breed.

If he noticed my bewilderment, it didn't show on his face.

"He must have liked it more than I ever did, Miri," he said.

"He must have, for you to be slavering after him like a bitch in heat after only one night..."

That fury expanded off him as he said it, making me flinch. His voice dropped to a murmur, almost intimate where he spoke into my ear.

"...Personally, I preferred screwing your human friends. They may be a lesser race...but at least they know their place. That one friend of yours? Lacey? She cried afterwards. She cried and cried. Silly, stupid cunt thought she'd betrayed you..."

Fighting his grip, I yanked on his fingers, trying to get more air into my lungs.

He's going to kill me. Ian's going to kill me.

It was the only thought that mattered.

I had to get free. I had to get him to let go of my throat before I blacked out. Nothing else mattered. Nothing else mattered at all.

I had to figure out what he needed to hear to let me live.

Or just loosen his hand enough that I could draw a full breath.

Looking down at me, he laughed.

"You still don't get it, do you, Miri? I don't care anymore. I would have killed you years ago, but it wasn't my decision. It was *never* my decision. I am but a soldier in a much larger army... you would have been dead minutes after I met you, had it been up to me." He squeezed my throat tighter, smiling when I let out a frightened cry, even as satisfaction exuded from his fingers. "But I don't fucking care anymore, Miri. I don't care. They can demote me, put me back in the trenches, kill me...I don't care. I'll take the penalty. Whatever it is, I'll take it. I don't give a shit. Whatever it is...it'll be worth it."

His smile widened, even as his eyes grew flat as metal.

245

"I'll consider it a public service..." That disgust returned to his blue eyes. "My boss thought you were harmless. He thought we could just keep you...like a little halfbreed pet. He assigned *me* to hold your leash." Fury once more twisted his face. "But I'm overruling him, love. I think he's wrong. The fact that you apparently like to screw *traitors to the race* strikes me as pretty compelling evidence that you're not as 'harmless' as you pretend..."

When I met his gaze, I recognized that dead-eyed stare.

My mind flickered back to the night before.

The museum burning.

The gun pointed at my face. The hatred I'd felt.

Even so, some part of me could scarcely make sense of it. Emotion hit me. Grief. More than that, confusion roiled my brain, fighting the adrenaline that kept screaming at me that I was about to die. I couldn't compute what my mind already knew, couldn't make sense of any of it. All I could think was that I was going to die. Ian was going to kill me.

The man I was going to marry was going to kill me.

"Why?" I gasped, barely able to get the word out under his vice-like grip. "Why?"

"*Gaos*," he said, staring at me with utter contempt. "It's really not an act with you, is it, Miriam? You really don't have a fucking clue about anything, do you?"

When I didn't answer, gasping and clawing at his hands around my throat, he shook me, violently enough to make my teeth rattle. My throat burned. Every sliver of oxygen I managed to get down it felt like not enough, not nearly enough.

I hit out at him sharply with my elbows and feet, but he smashed my head against the wall again. It terrified me how close I came to blacking out that time.

"You okay, doc?" she said softly.

I smiled at that, I couldn't help it. Raising the coffee cup to my lips, I took a long drink. Then, thinking about her question, I nodded.

"I am, actually," I said, some surprise in my voice. "More or less."

"More or less?"

When I glanced up, Angel looked skeptical.

After watching me a few seconds longer, she only nodded, though, and somehow, I got the sense I'd reassured her in some way. Leaning her elbows on the table, she let out a longer-sounding sigh.

"I could sleep for a week myself," she said, almost like she heard my thoughts. She sighed again, smoothing her braids. "But I'm not sure I could sleep at all right now, either."

"Yeah." I shifted my weight around slightly on the gray chair, tugging the blanket tighter around me. "Me too."

Another silence fell between us. Then Angel looked back at me, her eyes holding a denser scrutiny.

"He's waiting, you know. He hasn't left."

"Who?" I said, puzzled.

She let out a snort, rolling her eyes. "Who do you think, girlfriend?"

My mind remained totally blank.

"Black," Angel said, shaking her head, her eyes bemused. "Quentin Black. He's waiting for you. Or he was when I last saw."

I looked around in surprise at the empty conference room. "So?" I said. "Why isn't he here then?"

"Nick made him wait outside," Angel said, smiling faintly. "He said he couldn't see you for 'medical' reasons...and because you're no longer any kind of suspect, Black couldn't bully us with his lawyers. I think Nick's just being petty."

I shook my head, setting down the coffee cup and folding my arms, hugging the blanket to my chest. Even so, I let out an involuntary laugh.

"Men," I said, my bleak humor bleeding into weariness. "I'm beginning to think Nick and Black just need to find a private room somewhere to compare their Jack Johnson's...see who has the biggest and prettiest one and just get it over with."

Angel laughed aloud at that.

I was heartened to hear it, especially since it was a real laugh.

When I glanced over at her, she grinned at me.

"Agreed," she said. "Maybe we could have a betting pool?"

"Maybe," I grunted. Feeling another wave of tiredness wash over me, I sunk lower in my chair, wincing when I jarred my leg. "Can I go home, Angel? Please?"

Angel let out a sigh. "It's still a crime scene, Miri. You might need to get a hotel." She hesitated, studying my eyes. "Or you could come stay with me."

Seeing the sincerity there, and feeling a faint whisper of guilt off her, it occurred to me that she was afraid I wouldn't want to stay with her. Not after she and Nick accused me of being involved in the bombing the night before, and peripherally at least, the murders. She felt guilty for dragging me in here like a regular suspect.

More than that, she felt guilty for doubting me.

Looking at her, I wanted to reassure her, but I wasn't sure how to do it right. That conversation might have to wait until I'd gotten some real sleep too.

I laid a hand on her arm though, smiling at her.

"I really think I need a hotel this time," I told her. "I need about a week of being a hermit...and I know if I go to your place, we'll be up all night with a bottle of tequila. Or two. I'm thinking we should raincheck the heavy drinking and girl-talk part of my recovery until after I've pulled my brain off the floor and stuck it partway back in my head..."

Angel let out an involuntary laugh, but she nodded.

I felt relief on her, too, enough that I knew she sensed the subtext of what I was trying to tell her. Meaning that she and I were all right.

And we were all right, I realized.

"Too true, doc," she smiled, giving me a rueful look. Nodding towards the door to the conference room then, she grinned wider. "All right. Well, in that case, I'll let you field any other offers you might have. Concerning places to stay."

"Other offers?" I frowned in puzzlement.

She laughed. "You heard me, right? He's waiting for you out there," she said, motioning towards the door as she rose to her feet. Smiling down at me, I saw curiosity touch her brown eyes. "He has been for hours, Miri. I think that sends a message all of its own, don't you?"

I pursed my lips, staring at the door.

"I seriously doubt it," I said.

She laughed again, helping me to my feet.

Even so, I found myself swallowing a second later, as I turned over her words.

I knew exactly what she was talking about, I realized.

265

I'D BARELY MET HIS GAZE WHEN HE FROWNED, HIS GOLD EYES FLICKING down me in the hospital gear and the SFPD sweatshirt I'd borrowed from Angel after they bandaged up my arms. I'd already given back the blanket, just prior to entering the public waiting area of the station.

Before the door closed behind me, he rose smoothly to his feet, all six-foot-whatever of him.

I couldn't help noticing he was back to his previous uniform of black pants, a black, form-fitting T-shirt and what looked like motorcycle boots. It didn't do much for my resolve, seeing him staring at me like that, or the tattoos on display on his arms.

Even so, the look on his face wasn't hard to interpret.

"No," he said, before I'd even opened my mouth. "Absolutely not."

I exhaled, staring up at him in disbelief. "I haven't said anything yet, Black."

"You aren't staying in a *fucking* hotel," he growled.

I looked at Angel, who let out an involuntary-seeming laugh. Patting me on the back, she gave me a sympathetic smile when I glanced at her.

"You're on your own here, doc," she told me. "You're the one who made friends with the psycho."

"We're not—" I began angrily.

"Employer, actually," Black cut in, giving Angel a measured look. "She works for me, and I have an obligation to protect my investment. And as an asset of Black Securities and Investigations, Ms. Fox has an obligation to let me."

Angel burst out in a real laugh at that.

She didn't comment though, just waved us off, like she thought both of us were off our rockers. I knew she was busy with the case, that she'd been on babysitting duty with me long enough, so I didn't call her back, but only bit my lip, watching her leave.

When I faced Black, he was looking me over again.

"I've already got you a room," he said.

"What the hell does that mean?" I said, incredulous.

"You know what it means." His eyes hardened. "It's a separate room. The door locks."

I shook my head, folding my arms. "No."

"Then at one of my other properties. With my security, Miriam."

"*One* of your properties?" I said in disbelief. "Just how many 'properties' do you have?"

"Enough." His cat-like eyes didn't waver. "I'll give you brochures to choose from," he added. "But I think we can leave that for tomorrow, don't you? Today you'll get a room in the building on California..." Seeing the protest building in my eyes, he cut in, holding up a hand. "...A *separate* room, Miriam. As in a separate apartment. Not mine. You can even put a chair up against the door handle to keep me out if you want."

Staring up at him, I felt my resistance wavering.

Moreover, I had an irrational desire to laugh again.

More to the point, I didn't really think he was going to attack me if I went with him. Then again, I wasn't entirely sure it was him I didn't trust. Not only him.

Even as I thought it, he stepped closer to me, his hands on his hips.

"Humor me for tonight. If we reach an understanding about employment, we can discuss more permanent living arrangements. Assuming you want to move out of your current place."

I thought about that too, frowning.

But it was too soon to go into all that.

It was too soon for me to even think about the possibility of working for Black full time, much less whatever else might be going on between us.

Looking up at him, I realized it was too late, too.

Sighing, I found myself nodding, almost before I knew I meant to.

It seemed to be a pattern with us. Already.

"All right," I said, exhaling in defeat. "Okay. Tonight."

His expression didn't move after I spoke.

Even so, I swear I felt something deeper in him relax.

Watching him turn, aiming his feet for the door of the station without bothering to check to see if I followed, I knew, without a doubt, that either way, I was definitely in trouble.

Continue reading about Quentin Black and Miri Fox with:

BLACK AS NIGHT
Quentin Black Mystery #2

If you enjoyed the book please consider leaving a review on the vendor site where you purchased it. A short review is fine and greatly appreciated. Word of mouth is essential for any author to succeed.

THE QUENTIN BLACK WORLD encompasses a number of dark, gritty paranormal mystery arcs with science fiction elements, starring brilliant and mysterious Quentin Black and forensic psychologist Miriam Fox. For fans of realistic paranormal mysteries with romantic elements, the series spans continents and dimensions as Black solves crimes, takes on other races and tries to keep his and Miri's true identities secret to keep them both alive.

THE BRIDGE & SWORD WORLD is a dark, unique and gritty apocalyptic world and alternate history of Earth. It features a young woman grappling with her role in bringing about the end of one world and the start of a new one. Follow Allie Taylor and her antihero partner in crime, Dehgoies Revik, as they fight terrifying enemies and one another in a passionate story spanning centuries, and filled with unpredictable twists, turns and betrayals.

THE GATE SHIFTER SERIES is an unusual shifter romance centering on shifters from another world altogether, called morph. Earth humans remained blissfully ignorant of the existence of alternate dimensions until Nihkil Jamri tries to save private detective, Dakota Reyes, while he is surveying Earth.

THE ALIEN APOCALYPSE SERIES is a post-apocalyptic dystopian romance about a tough girl named Jet Tetsuo who grew up on Earth following an alien invasion. Forced into living among her conquerors, she must learn to navigate a treacherous world full of enemies who pose as friends, even as she becomes their most famous fighter in the Rings, their modern day version of the coliseum where she must fight just to survive.

For more books by JC Andrijeski, visit www.jcandrijeski.com
"Seeking Truth in Made-Up Worlds"

About the Author

JC Andrijeski is a *USA Today* bestselling author who writes paranormal mystery, along with apocalyptic and cyberpunk-y science fiction, often with a metaphysical bent.

JC has a background in journalism, history and politics, and currently occupies herself by traipsing around the globe and reading whatever she can get her hands on. She grew up in the Bay Area of California, but has lived abroad in Europe, Australia and Asia, and from coast to coast in the continental United States.

She currently lives and writes full time in Bangkok, Thailand.

To learn more about JC and her writing, please visit jcandrijeski.com.

For an automatic email when JC's next book is released, join THE REBEL ARMY at http://hyperurl.co/JCA-Newsletter

More Books by JC Andrijeski

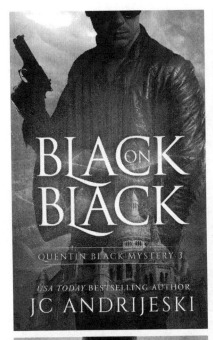

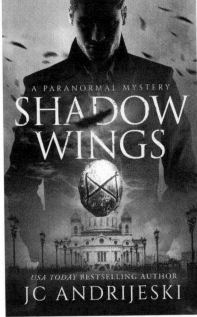

85747429R00171

Made in the USA
San Bernardino, CA
22 August 2018